To Die, or Not to Die . . .

To Die, or Not to Die...

A John Darnell Mystery

Sam McCarver

Five Star • Waterville, Maine

First Edition
First Printing: August 2003

Published in 2003 in conjunction with
Tekno Books and Ed Gorman.

Set in 11 pt. Plantin.

Printed in the United States on permanent paper.

Library of Congress Cataloging-in-Publication Data

McCarver, Sam.
   To die, or not to die—: a John Darnell mystery /
Sam McCarver.—1st ed.
      p. cm.—(Five Star first edition mystery series)
   ISBN 0-7862-5444-0 (hc : alk. paper)
   1. Darnell, John (Fictitious character)—Fiction.
2. Stratford-upon-Avon (England)—Fiction.   3. Drama
festivals—Fiction.   4. Theater—Fiction.   5. Actors—
Fiction.   I. Title.   II. Series.
PS3563.C337425T6 2003
813'.6—dc21   2003052851

For my family.

"Double, double toil and trouble;
Fire burn and cauldron bubble."

Macbeth, Act IV, Scene I
William Shakespeare

Author's Note

This sixth novel in my John Darnell Mystery Series features John Darnell and his wife, Penny, in another exciting adventure, this time solving murders in the year 1919 in Stratford-upon-Avon, England, the birthplace of William Shakespeare, during the 150th anniversary of the annual Shakespeare festival. As in each book in this series, I include real people of the era who were involved in literature or the arts at the time.

In this book, John Barrymore, the most exciting and handsome American actor of the day, thirty-seven years of age and unmarried, comes to England to act in two Shakespeare plays in Stratford, and is featured in the story. The famous, aging stage actresses, Sarah Bernhardt and Ellen Terry, also appear on stage. However, except as to certain general aspects of their lives, their participation in this story derives strictly from my imagination, since this "history-mystery" is a work of fiction, in which my characters become real people and real people become my characters.

I thank Ed Gorman and John Helfers for their encouragement and enthusiasm and express my appreciation to all the excellent staff of Five Star for their reviews of the manuscript and great artwork in producing this new John Darnell mystery for your enjoyment.

Prologue

Stratford-upon-Avon, England

The flickering light of the candles cast giant shadows of the scribe on the bare walls of the room—ghostly images evoking those that later would inspire wonder and awe that night as actors strutted and fretted upon a stage, speaking the bard's words, as he would wish, trippingly on their tongues. The writer bent over his work with quill pen in hand, dipping it frequently into the small jar of ink and scratching words onto the page.

On occasion, he referred to finished pages laid out on the desk. And as he wrote certain passages, a faint smile sometimes fluttered on his lips, at once crinkling the edges of his eyes and softening his cool features. At intervals, he quaffed wine from a beaker, sitting back for minutes at a time with a faraway look, his mind distant, in another time and place. Afterward he grasped the quill with renewed vigor and continued his task.

By the time he finished the job he had assigned himself for the night, the two tapers on his desk had burned low, as had the fire in the fireplace. He spread out his last sheets on the desktop to dry and returned the quill and corked-up ink bottle to a drawer. Wetting his fingertips, he pinched out one of the candles, picked up the other candlestick holder, and surveyed the papers on his desk with satisfaction. For the first time, he became aware of the pounding rain outside, so lost he had been in his ruminations and writings.

He stepped toward the door, but, following every artist's instinct for a traditional, last appreciation of his work, he turned back to gaze with pride at the final sheets he had written and allowed a tight smile to brighten his serious appearance. *Another masterpiece,* he thought.

At the top of the first page, the ornate signature, replete with flourishes and flairs, stared back at the inscriber, striking and trenchant, as if endorsing his self-satisfied assessment of the long night's work. The signature read . . . *Wm. Shakespeare.*

Chapter One

London, England, Saturday, June 21, 1919

Professor John Darnell put down his sherry glass and reached quickly for the jangling telephone, hoping it would not wake his wife, Penny, who had already gone up to their bedroom. Just entering her final eight weeks before the expected delivery of her first child, although still very active, she had taken to retiring early sometimes, leaving Darnell to pore over old books and sip a bit of sherry in the sitting room before going up himself. A telephone call at this hour was rare, and, when one came, often indicated the beginnings of a new case. What was it this time?

"Darnell, here," he said into the phone.

"Professor, this is Mayor Aylmer of Stratford-upon-Avon. Chief Inspector Bruce Howard of Scotland Yard referred me to you."

The man's voice reflected agitation. Darnell knew that from the first words. But Stratford-upon-Avon? The home of William Shakespeare? Not a place, he thought, likely to generate much commotion or turbulence. But Chief Inspector Howard's connection put a potential criminal dimension on the call.

"Bruce Howard? Yes. Fine man. And how can I help you, Mayor?"

The mayor rushed on, his voice now revealing more anxiety as he explained his purpose. "You're known as a debunker of the supernatural, the chief inspector told me. Apparitions, jinxes, ghosts?"

"Yes, go on."

"We have them here. Twice now, the people in town have sighted ghosts. The first time—well, I thought it was a prank, a hoax, you know. But tonight, the ghost was seen again, just an hour ago. I called Howard, the only man I know at the Yard, and he put me onto you. I met him some years ago when he visited Stratford with his family."

"Tell me what people think they saw." Darnell had long since ceased being surprised at reports of apparitions. Getting the raw facts, he found, offered the best opportunities for understanding the source of the supposed supernatural happenings.

"We're in the midst of the Shakespeare festival, with plays every week. It's the sesquicentennial—a hundred and fifty years since the first festival in 1769. A tourist saw what he called a ghost as he walked home after a visit to a pub, following the Wednesday night play, *The Tempest*. And tonight, after *A Midsummer Night's Dream*, a local woman saw the thing." He paused. "The man didn't have too much ale, if that's what you're thinking, and the woman is our own tour guide. Very reliable."

"All right. But describe the apparition, please."

"Both descriptions matched. Clothing like you'd find on the ghost in *Hamlet*, or Banquo in *Macbeth*. Shakespearian. The face was white, pasty, ghost-like. Bloodless lips, they said. With the apparent ability to just disappear in a blink of an eye."

"So, you're looking for advice? I'd say, first, that ghosts were quite commonplace in Shakespeare's plays, and it could just be a friendly hoax. Someone with a sense of humor. Festivals might lead to that sort of thing. Maybe one of your actors, having a bit of fun . . ."

"But this has got to stop, Professor! In two days, the famous actor, John Barrymore, comes here from America.

He's going to star in *Macbeth* next Thursday and *Hamlet* on Saturday. *Ghosts!* That will infuriate him."

Darnell smiled. "He has to deal with them enough on-stage, I suppose, and wouldn't want them upstaging him around town."

"Stage actors are very sensitive."

"Why not give it a few days? Just keep watch, alert your constable. Perhaps you've seen the last of your, ah, ghosts."

"I can't take that chance. Can you imagine how Barrymore would feel if all the audiences could talk about was ghosts—and not his, well, great performances?"

"Yes—I see."

"Also, many people still believe in ghosts, and if word gets around, well, it might affect the festival. Professor, I'm asking you to come here and investigate."

"You realize it is very likely someone having fun at your expense?"

His tone became more intense. "Maybe, but I need to know what's happening. I can't have the festival disrupted, my star actor angry, tourists upset or worried. I—well, this has obviously never happened before, and we can't deal with it." He paused. "We'd put you up, of course, our festival coffers would allow for your fee, a very reasonable one, and you'd be able to see John Barrymore perform in *Macbeth* and *Hamlet*. You'd be here not over a week, because Barrymore leaves next Sunday."

Darnell thought of Penny, seven months along towards birth of their first child. "I'll consider it overnight, Mayor, call you in the morning."

"I'd need you tomorrow. You'd need a day to meet people and look about before Barrymore arrives Monday."

"I can't promise you now. But if I can come, I could make it by tomorrow night if I leave in the morning."

13

"We'd pick you up at the train station." The mayor gave Darnell his telephone number and said, with an edge of desperation, Darnell thought, "The success of the entire festival may depend on your coming."

Darnell hung up the receiver and finished his sherry. He stared into the dying fire in the fireplace and thought of Penny. He'd carefully planned to allow no cases or teaching assignments to take him out of town for the next two months. He wanted to be with Penny. The most important event in their lives since they met and married seven years ago was almost upon them—their first child. Nothing must complicate that. Walking to the stairs and up to their bedroom, he resolved he'd simply tell Penny about it in the morning and explain that, although he hadn't yet declined the mayor's urgings, he felt the festival would have to do without him.

Breakfast seemed the best time to bring it up. They had arisen and finished an early meal, and he was enjoying his second cup of coffee as he explained the proposition the mayor had put forth on the phone. "I can't go, of course. I just gave him the courtesy of saying I'd sleep on it. One or two ghosts, more or less, is unimportant with what we're looking forward to in August. Just wanted you to know."

A frown creased Penny's clear forehead and her violet eyes looked straight into his. "John, I hope you're not using me as an excuse. August is a long way off. One week? That's not much. And John Barrymore!"

"No. I couldn't leave you here."

"Leave me? But John, I'd go with you! Do you think I'd miss the chance to see John Barrymore act? Do you know what this means? It's history—the first time he'll act in a Shakespeare play."

"You'd go? But Penny . . ." His orderly thoughts, his decision to turn down the case, disrupted, thoughts swirled. "The train ride—your doctor—I don't know, Penny."

She laughed. "I'm not a patient—just an expectant mother. But it'll be fine. One week and we're back home."

Darnell poured more coffee and held back on responding for a moment. He thought of their adventures together, on the *Titanic*, in the lifeboats, on the *Carpathia*, and later on the *Orient Express*, of her bravery in the Ripper case and the Paris hotel murders. Penny had survived many adventures and much danger, and had helped him in his investigations, yes— but this time things were different. Two more months . . . He realized he was shaking his head, when he heard her speak again.

"John, let this be my decision. I don't think I could stand having you sit around this flat for two solid months with nothing to do. You can't stop living your life. And, besides . . ." she smiled as she laid a hand on his arm persuasively, ". . . I really want to see John Barrymore! Are you jealous? Is that it?"

"No, I—well, if your doctor approves it, we'll go, if you insist. But we'd have to leave as soon as we can pack."

"Good! Then get Dr. Raleigh on the phone and we'll both talk with him." She put her arm around his shoulder. "I know you're concerned, John, but it'll be all right. I'm sure of it."

Two hours later as they sat in their train compartment, looking out at the passing countryside, Penny said, "We couldn't have made the train without Sung. I can't believe we're actually going to Stratford. Seven years in England and you've never taken me there." She looked peevishly at her husband.

"And I'm not sure I should be doing it now," Darnell said, matching her tone. "Now if you feel discomfort . . ."

She laughed lightly. "I know. You'll send me home. Don't worry."

Darnell sighed and took her hand in his. "I'm a worrier, I admit it. I don't know how else to play the role of expectant father."

"Role, yes. That reminds me of the plays. I do hope your case is not solved before Saturday. I want to see both of them, but especially *Hamlet* Saturday night."

"You want to see Barrymore in it."

"Exactly. 'The Great Profile' they call him, and with good reason. Everyone in America who knows anything about the stage knows about the Barrymore brothers and sister. Their father, Maurice, was an actor before them. And I've been following reviews of performances of Lionel, Ethel, and John in the *Times* over the years."

Darnell smiled. "I think if you'd had another career it would have been acting—I know you did some in America."

She nodded. "Amateur stage plays. Mostly in Texas. One or two in New York." Her violet eyes twinkled. "But my greatest performance was in London two years ago. Bernard Shaw said it was great, didn't he?"

John Darnell shuddered. "Your career might have ended in Whitechapel—and your life."

"Well, I won't be doing any acting here. And I think I'll be perfectly safe from your Stratford-upon-Avon ghost. You said even the mayor thinks someone is putting on an act."

Darnell nodded, but did not join in her light mood. "There are no ghosts, although some would like us to believe there are. But the fact that they want us to believe it—that's worrisome in itself. What possible reason could someone have for scaring the good people of Stratford?"

Penny Darnell looked in her husband's eyes. "Whatever reason it is, John, I'm sure you'll find it out."

She linked her arm comfortably in his and leaned back in her seat, looking out at trees and fields that moved swiftly by them. She breathed deeply, and her eyelids closed, opened again, and closed once more in sleep. John Darnell looked at her, thinking how radiant her face had become in these final weeks before she would give birth. And he thought of Stratford. And the ghost.

Chapter Two

Stratford-upon-Avon, Sunday, June 22

Blake Aylmer looked the part of a mayor. The three-piece suit with a gold watch-chain and fob, which spread across the vest from one pocket to the other, accentuated the girth of his midsection. He boasted a full head of wavy gray hair. The gold-rimmed glasses and mother-of-pearl-topped cane completed it. Yes, Darnell thought, the mayor fit the role perfectly.

"Professor and Mrs. Darnell," the mayor said heartily. "I hope you had a good trip." He looked with undisguised surprise at Penny's rounded form. "Mrs. Darnell? Are you comfortable?"

"Yes, Mayor." Penny smiled. "I'm very durable."

The two men shook hands, and the mayor said, "I see you'll soon be due for congratulations."

"In August," Darnell said. He smiled at Penny. "My wife insisted on coming along."

The mayor laughed. "Women do get their way. My wife, for instance. She insisted on arranging your rooms for you herself. Went to the Anne Hathaway Inn, and made them give her the front suite for you. You'll like it."

"Thank you," Penny said. "I'd like to meet your wife."

"You will." He beamed. "We've arranged a supper for you within the hour at the Inn, not far from here. Some of the theater people, my wife, and myself. A small affair, good food, conversation. Then you'll probably want to retire early."

"After the train trip and the ride here from the station in the car you sent for us—and thanks for that—we'll probably

18

fit into that schedule very nicely." Darnell paused. "But you and I need to take some time tonight to talk about this case."

Aylmer nodded gravely. "After we take the meal, we'll do that. You'll meet some people that can help you, at supper."

"I'll break in our rooms while you talk," Penny said.

"The Inn is just one block from here." Mayor Aylmer looked at Penny. "I like the fact that my office is in the center of the town's activities, near the inns, the restaurants, and very close to the theater."

"I can walk the block, Mayor," Penny said. "And a lot more than that. She smiled. " 'Lay on . . . Macduff.' "

"Ten minutes in Stratford and the lady quotes Shakespeare."

Mayor Aylmer laughed and said, "Follow me to the Hathaway, then. The supper's at eight, and you'll just have time to freshen up before that."

They found the rooms as comfortable as Mayor Aylmer had suggested, with a view to the street below from the second story, a massive bedroom, a bathroom on the same scale, and a sitting room with fireplace, well-stocked bookshelves and wine rack.

After they dressed for dinner—Darnell taking an extra shave for the occasion and Penny changing into a long dress that picked up the color of her long auburn hair and had been tailored for her present condition—they descended the curved staircase from the second floor to the first, then crossed the spacious lobby to the dining room.

Guests of the Inn, tourists, and locals who had dropped in for a pint occupied settees and corner arrangements of plush couches and chairs. They watched with obvious interest as Darnell and Penny proceeded across the room—the six-foot tall, trim and straight, well-dressed Englishman and his stately wife.

"We're making a bit of a scene, John," Penny said.

He smiled. "We're entitled. Just look straight ahead and you won't blush."

"I haven't blushed in years." She laughed, but felt color come to her cheeks.

As they entered the dining room, the mayor walked over to them, leaving an elegantly-gowned lady in the company of a tall man with dark brown hair and a handsome face suitable, Darnell thought, for the stage. "Come," Aylmer said. "Meet my wife and the director of our plays."

When he introduced his wife, Kimberley, she said to Penny, "You may call me Kim, my dear. I'm going to take you under my wing while you're here. Your husband may be very busy."

The man with her introduced himself to them, holding out a hand to Darnell. "Rex Flint," he said. "Glad you're here. Sit next to me at the table so we can talk." He looked around the room conspiratorially. "There may be some here who'd like to hear what I want to say, I'm sure." He nodded at a rectangular table at the far end of the room in an alcove. "We'll be sitting there. My wife will be joining us, along with some other people associated with the theater or the town's affairs."

Aylmer provided Darnell with a glass of sherry, and Penny took a sarsaparilla. They stood near the bar and surveyed their surroundings. The room buzzed with conversation. Darnell wondered what secrets Flint intended to disclose.

Darnell glanced at diners in the largely-filled room, tables of two or four typically, apparently in the best clothing they'd brought on their tourist trip. The light in the room had been softened, for atmosphere, and candles burned at each table.

They walked to the table reserved for them which, because of the alcove, provided privacy for them to talk freely of the case.

"Here come the others," Aylmer said to Darnell, who noticed that Aylmer's wife had taken Penny to one side and engaged her in spirited conversation. Seeing Darnell's line of vision, Aylmer said, "We have three children, all grown now. Kim's probably giving her motherly advice."

Three women and two men came up to the table. A redhaired woman in a glittering gown took Flint's arm possessively and said, "Introduce me, Rex. Where are your manners?"

Rex Flint and Mayor Aylmer assisted each other in the process, stumbling quickly through introductions of Darnell and his wife to the others—first, Mrs. Glenna Flint, who had shown her ownership of her husband to all. Then Felicia Baron, an actress blessed, Darnell thought, with a luxuriant quantity of long, brown hair and emerald green eyes.

They met the others. Mrs. Anne Burgh, shy, respectful and attentive. A widow, the mayor told Darnell, with a young daughter away at school, Anne was a long-time Stratford tour guide. Richard Latimer, of average height but putting on weight and losing his black hair, produced the plays and sponsored the Shakespeare festival. Darnell sized him up as having enough money not to worry about budgets. Johanna Latimer, his quiet wife, was one whom some might be tempted privately to call mousey. Darnell felt the slim and diminutive woman in her late thirties was a complete opposite to Glenna Flint—she, with a desire for privacy, Glenna with a need to be a star—at least in her husband's eyes.

They all took seats at the table. As the conversation resumed, he realized he'd begun his detecting already—trying to read the emotions and psychology of the newcomers in the first few minutes of their acquaintance. Professors of psychology and philosophy were inclined, he knew, to do that, and coupled with his extra career, investigating not only crimes but evidences of possible paranormal activities, it was perfectly natural.

He smiled across at Penny, placed next to Kimberley Aylmer, who was listening to her speak. Penny nodded at Darnell, as if she knew he was already at his work. She could see he was plunging into the mystery of a new case that would soon deepen, and was alert for suspects. But in her situation, with John's attentiveness, she knew he'd be equally alert now for her needs.

The dinner met their greatest anticipation. English fare on the menu, roast beef and chops, dishes which Darnell doted on, equal to the cooking abilities of Sung, who had become master of quite an English menu in the Darnell household. Friendly conversation among the women, all of whom were quite taken with Penny and her expectations. Everything but information that Darnell really wanted from Aylmer, who sat at the other end of the table.

But what he heard from Rex Flint in the conversations they struck up gave him enough to occupy his thoughts, and might help to relate in some way to his other inquiries. Soon, dishes were cleared away and they were all enjoying coffee, some desserts.

"I know why you're here," Flint said, in a voice low enough not to be heard by the others who were speaking vigorously about plays and play-acting. "I know you're investigating Aylmer's ghosts. I'll let him go into that with you. But two other things you should hear about as a backdrop to this. I don't know how they're related, but I suppose that's your specialty—to piece them together."

"Depends on what they are," Darnell said. "I'm listening."

Flint nodded. "First, the drowned cats."

"Dead cats?"

"Yes. *Drowned cats.* They were found in the river, three of them, in a sack weighted down—but with not quite enough weight—and snagged by a boy's fishpole. Shouldn't have been fishing anyway, but there you have it. If he hadn't been, we might not have found the cats."

"And what do drowned cats mean to you? Something special? Or just a vicious act by an immature individual?"

"Iago said it in *Othello.* '*Don't drown yourself, Rodrigo,*' Iago said, . . . '*drown cats.*' *Othello* played the night before."

"When were the cats found?"

"A week ago Sunday. I'm not surprised something like this ghost has come along now."

Darnell mused on the information. "He seems to be following your playbook. First, *Othello.* Then ghosts, maybe precursors to *Macbeth* and *Hamlet.*"

"The mayor didn't regard the cats as important as I do. I think it was the first of several strange incidents. The two ghost sightings were the second and third."

"And there was another?"

"I haven't mentioned it to Blake. He's been worried about the ghost sightings. A heavy curtain weight fell in rehearsals a few days ago and almost hit an actress. Her name is Portia Regan. If it had struck her, it could have killed her. It might have been an accident, of course, but along with everything else that's been happening . . ."

"The mayor needs to know about that."

"He will, tomorrow. You're hearing it first only because I'm sitting next to you."

Darnell said, "Tell me what attitude people took toward the dead—to be specific, the *drowned cats?*"

"Not many know about it. The mayor didn't want to make

too much of it. He doesn't want to exaggerate matters, to alarm the tourists."

"And who knows about the weight falling?"

"Several actors and actresses on stage, and the producer."

Darnell was silent for a moment, looking about the table. The meal over, he found Penny's gaze upon him from across the table as she looked away from Mrs. Aylmer and raised an eyebrow.

Darnell said, "We'll tell the mayor tomorrow. I'll be coming over to the theater in the morning." He stood and walked over to Penny. He spoke to the mayor for a moment. Then to Penny he said, "Shall we go up dear? It's been a long day."

Penny stood, and after a flurry of goodnights, the two retraced their steps across a rather deserted lobby, up the stairs, and into their room. Making sure Penny had everything she needed, Darnell said, "I promised the mayor I'd meet him in the lounge in a few minutes to discuss the case. I won't be long, I promise." He kissed her lightly.

Penny yawned. "I'll be asleep. Don't worry."

Darnell found the mayor sitting by himself at the bar in a lounge almost as deserted as the lobby. One couple sat in a corner booth. Two men huddled at the other end of the bar. He and Aylmer ordered sherry and carried their glasses to a table at a distance from the other patrons and took seats. Darnell thanked him again for the dinner and hotel arrangements, and said he was anxious to plunge into the case.

He lowered his voice, "Tell me more about your ghosts, Mayor." He paused. "And anything else you think I should know."

"I see Flint has been telling you about the cats. I didn't want to mention that on the phone. It's too bizarre."

Darnell nodded.

"We can't allow all of this to get around town. Tourists won't like it. Only a few know about the two ghost sightings, and that's bad enough. I want to keep it that way."

"Flint knows all about the ghosts?"

"Yes. Also the constable, my wife, the tourist, and our tour guide, Anne, who saw the person masquerading as a ghost. The theater night watchman, Skelton. And the boy fishing who found the cats. But no others know what's been happening. I'm hoping you can solve this before news of these things spreads."

"I'm glad you believe it was 'masquerading.' You obviously don't believe in the supernatural either."

"No, but I know the damage that could result. I want this to go away before it gets worse. You must find out who's doing these things." He paused and looked surreptitiously around the room. "There's something else—not even Rex knows. I'm telling you in confidence. Don't tell your wife . . ."

Darnell said, "Sounds mysterious. All right. Mum's the word."

"An aide to the Prince of Wales called me yesterday after they heard about Barrymore coming. The Prince wants to see him perform Hamlet Saturday night. Here."

Darnell whistled low. "That is sticky. What're you going to tell them?"

"I held back on the ghost matter. I told him I'd contact him Friday and let him know whether we could provide enough security. He understands that word. I left it there."

"Good. Then that gives us at least four days. All right—tell me about the people you say witnessed the so-called ghosts."

"One was a young man, a tourist who had seen a play, stopped off at a pub, and walked home late Wednesday night.

25

He glimpsed the thing behind the playhouse."

"Why did he think to call it a ghost, specifically?"

"He admitted he thought at first it was only an actor, because of the clothing, but as he drew closer saw the pasty white face, and then the thing seemed to vanish. He ran toward where it had been standing and it was just gone. He told the constable about it, rather excitedly, and the constable told me."

"And the second?"

"It was last night about ten, an hour before I called you. Anne Burghe saw it. You've met her, a very reliable lady."

"The description?"

"The same. The face also led her to call it a ghost."

Darnell thought a minute. "The ghosts in your plays—the King in *Hamlet*, Banquo in *Macbeth*. Did they look like them?"

"As to clothing, yes. But onstage faces of ghosts are made up in a very pale gray. These faces were described as white."

Darnell said, "We've covered all we can tonight. I'll see Flint at the theater tomorrow. We have to pool our information."

The mayor nodded. "All except the part about the Prince, of course. That's between you and me. They'll be doing rehearsals at the theater. And John Barrymore will arrive tomorrow."

"Then I'll meet you down here in the lobby in the morning, say, at nine. And we'll walk over to the theater."

Mayor Aylmer stood and yawned. "My wife will see after yours. Make sure that she gets breakfast and lunch, show her some of the town. Anne Burghe, the guide, will be with them."

They shook hands. Darnell watched the mayor walk out the front door of the lobby as he strode to the stairs and up them to their room. He knew Penny would be asleep at this hour, almost midnight. For the first time, he felt comfortable about having brought her with him. She'd meet Barrymore and see Shakespeare's plays.

Also, it would be something notable for both of them to remember about the last two months before his son—or could it be a daughter?—was born. In coming years, they'd have something to tell him about these days. As he unlocked their door he smiled, realizing that more and more he was finding himself using the masculine pronoun regarding their child, instead of the feminine. Was it a sign? He shook his head and said to himself, *Darnell, you're becoming superstitious!*

Chapter Three

Southampton, Monday, June 23

John Barrymore looked down with satisfaction at the Southampton dock as the *Mauretania* slowly eased into its mooring. He had enjoyed relaxing during the fast trip on Cunard's speediest ocean liner, fully relaxed now, escaped from the regimen of his continuous performances as the sexual but effeminate Giannetto in the stage play, *The Jest*, which had set box-office records since its tumultuous opening in April.

Barrymore felt renewed by the voyage, thankful the play had closed for the summer, and looking forward to the hiatus from his role as his work in the Shakespeare festival would provide. *Shakespeare!* He smiled at the mere thought of the name. This would be his first essay into the realm of the great bard, but he felt certain his private rehearsals of his title roles in *Macbeth* and *Hamlet* the past three months had prepared him.

With his valet, Brandon, at his shoulder and both of them at the rail peering into the crowd of faces below, now ever nearer as the ship sought its assigned slot along the pier, he murmured the line that hadn't left his mind during the trip from New York—

"To be, or not to be . . ."

"Sir?" Brandon said, looking at him. "Do you wish something?"

Barrymore smiled. "Yes, Brandon. I do. I wish to be in Stratford, so we can renew our rehearsals. Do you realize I go on stage with *Macbeth* in just four nights?"

"Yes, sir."

Barrymore sniffed. "Of course, it's not my favorite. I'll leave that to Lionel for his use. It's *Hamlet* I want to do. That's Saturday night." He struck his right fist into his left palm. "All of this is just a prelude, you know. Someday, back in America . . ."

Brandon nodded. "You'll do Hamlet there."

"Yes, my friend." Barrymore stared down at the proceedings now that the ship had docked, the lowering of the ramps for the disembarkation of passengers. He spoke in a soft voice, as if to himself, ruminatively, looking ahead into the future, "And I'll be the best Hamlet there ever was—they'll say that about me."

"Yes, sir."

"The Prince of Denmark. *But not the sweet* Prince."

"No, sir?"

"I'll make him forceful, colloquial, dangerous, *Freudian*."

The purser's voice at his elbow brought his thoughts back to the present. "Mr. Barrymore, we moved your trunk and cases to the loading area, and a car has arrived for you from Stratford."

"Good, good! I'm anxious to get going. Brandon, if you'll just take that small case and bag of gifts . . ."

"Of course, sir."

They moved across the deck and down the stairs, wending their way through crowds of laughing and talking passengers, the purser leading the way. When they finally reached the ramp after a circuitous route through passengers preparing to disembark, Barrymore turned and placed some bills in the purser's hand. "You've been a great help. Thank you."

The purser pointed down the ramp at a gray-haired man in the black uniform of a chauffeur peering up at them, holding a large white card on which the name appeared in a large, bold scrawl: *John Barrymore.* "There's your driver," the

29

purser said. "You'll go by motorcar. The railway would take as long or longer, because it's not as direct. But it's a rather long trip by car."

Barrymore smiled. "Don't be concerned, my man. I want to see the countryside. This is my first visit to 'jolly old England' and I want to see a bit of her."

"You'll pass through Oxford." Then, with an air of reassurance, the purser added, "It's a closed car, I'm told."

John Barrymore waved a hand in the air, dismissing any negative thoughts. "We'll be fine, won't we Brandon?" He turned and marched down the disembarkation ramp toward the uniformed man, hand and arm outstretched in front of him, and his eyes sparkling. He felt as exhilarated as if he'd just managed a bottle of champagne by himself. The milk of human kindness, he thought, with some self-satisfaction, flowed freely in his veins today. *England, Shakespeare, and Hamlet! An actor's dream!*

Darnell and Mayor Aylmer walked the long block from the Anne Hathaway Inn at nine Monday morning after meeting in the lobby and taking a cup of coffee in the breakfast room. Darnell breathed deeply of the fresh air, which had a tinge of summer in it. He recalled the first and only time he had visited Stratford-upon-Avon, in his teen years with his father and mother. Only a tourist then, he now saw the town with a different perception, a sense that all was not well there.

Entering the large double-doored entrance, Aylmer led the way down the aisle to the stage, where the director sat in the front row keenly observing the actors. Hearing them approach, he held up a hand to those on stage and said in a loud voice, "We'll take a short break, now." He turned to the mayor and Darnell and shook hands with each.

The mayor said, "We won't interrupt you much, Rex. I

thought the professor would like to see the inside of the theater."

"More than that, I'll show you around. Give you a bit of a tour."

"I'd appreciate that," Darnell said.

Flint said to the mayor, "I have something to tell you."

The mayor looked from one to the other. "Another ghost sighting?"

Flint shook his head. "No. It happened last Wednesday afternoon, but I didn't have a chance to tell you yet."

"Five days ago? Then come out with it. Are you trying to make a greater mystery out of this?"

Flint said, "I'll show it to you. Come along." He led them around the side of the stage and up a few stairs to that level, then to the right to a prop storage area.

He pointed to the large gray object. "I left it here as we found it, so you could see it."

The mayor looked at it. "Is it a weight?"

"Exactly. For curtain raising. It fell and almost hit Portia Regan."

"She was at the table last night, but I didn't talk with her. She looked fine."

"Yes. It missed. She wouldn't look so fine if it had been a foot or two closer when it fell."

"Do you think it was other than an accident? Somebody did something deliberate?"

"I don't know. Maybe the professor can find out."

"Let's not make more of it, Rex, than it is. As far as we know it was an accident."

Flint nodded.

The mayor turned to Darnell. "We want your opinion, Professor."

"There seem to have been four strange events," Darnell

31

said. "The cat drowning was a cruel and deliberate act. The two ghost sightings could be hoaxes, are disruptive, but not dangerous in themselves. But this—if this was not an accident, we're looking at attempted murder. And that's very human and unghostlike."

"My fear is," the mayor said, "that if the public hears about them, they'll connect them."

Darnell asked him, "Then do you want police to investigate more definitively?"

The mayor shook his head vigorously. "If we asked for outside police, that would become known, and they'd probably just say there's no crime for them to investigate. We have our town constable, and he can handle what needs handling, without causing a stir. And your presence won't alarm anyone."

Darnell asked Flint, "Is the producer here?"

"Not right now. He's here for each performance and watches some rehearsals. Otherwise, he has a small office in the town center where he makes calls and meets people."

Mayor Aylmer nodded. "We'll see him today or tomorrow."

Darnell asked the director, "Would it bother anyone if I observed some of the rehearsals?"

Flint said, "You're welcome any time. I'll let the doorman and watchman know you'll be coming." He glanced at his watch. "Now let's finish our tour. Mostly dressing rooms and prop storage areas."

Darnell nodded. "Show me all the outside entrances. I'm interested in security over them. Just a matter of precaution."

After Darnell left for his visit to the theater, Penny Darnell finished the juice, egg, toast, and milk he'd ordered up for her. Still in her gown, she stood sideways and looked in the full-length mirror at her body's profile. Instinctively her two hands clasped together around her now very rounded midsection. At least twenty pounds now, she thought, maybe more. She sighed with the mixed feelings of loss of her slender form, yet the realization that the end of the long nine months would be soon, eight more weeks, more or less.

Anticipation fought concern as she looked forward to the event that would change forever her life and her husband's. They'd be parents, with responsibilities and experiences they could only imagine from what they'd read and learned from others. In times alone, like this, she'd think of her own mother who had died with her father in the train accident over ten years ago. Her thoughts always ended—*if only she could be here now* . . .

She tossed her hair back and took a breath. No time for that. She ran bathwater, turned to her suitcases while waiting, and laid out the clothes she planned to wear that day. Shortly before ten a.m., the appointed time for meeting the mayor's wife in the hotel lobby, she had finished her bath and dressed.

Descending the stairs into the lobby, she felt refreshed to see a bustle of activity. She took a seat on a couch and watched the front entrance for sight of Kimberley Aylmer. In only a few minutes, the mayor's wife walked briskly through the doorway and across the lobby, accompanied by Mrs. Anne Burghe, the tour guide Penny had met at the dinner table the night before. Although they had not spoken, she gained the impression the young widow was in her mid-thirties, and knew she was a young mother herself.

"Good morning, good morning," Kimberley Aylmer said in a bright voice. "I hope you slept well."

"Thank you. We're enjoying the rooms. Very comfortable."

"You know Mrs. Burghe . . ."

"Yes. Anne isn't it?"

The other woman nodded. "And Penny? I'm glad to be able to be with you this morning. No other tours scheduled today. So I'm all yours to help you see the town."

"Wonderful!"

Kimberley looked Penny up and down. "Are you set for some walking?"

"I need the exercise. My doctor says keep active."

Anne Burghe smiled. "We can supply the exercise. But we'll stop for lunch in a while. Mustn't overdo."

"John said he'd return about two or three. That would be fine."

Kimberley said, "We may see him while we're walking. This is really a small town. Not like London."

"I'm ready," Penny said, and tucked the long strap of her purse over her shoulder. "Let's go."

Anne Burghe seemed to take the lead, which was her usual role in touring, a step or two ahead of Penny and Kimberley Aylmer. They strolled slowly, walking down the sidewalk past the crystal and china shops, antique stores, souvenir shops, and other hotels and inns. They moved down Chapel Lane past the Shakespeare Memorial Theater, a Victorian Gothic building, a rounded and spired three-story main structure decorated at its front with statuary, including a tall tower and a large adjacent brick building, surrounded by expansive greenery and trees, all alongside the River Avon. Penny admired it, and looked about for any sign of her husband, concluding he was obviously inside.

"It was opened in 1879, forty years ago now," Anne Burghe said. "Beautiful, isn't it? A local man started a national campaign to finance the work. You'll enjoy seeing the interior, but we won't stop here just now," Anne said. "Professor Darnell may need this time for himself. We'll see it later."

Penny said, "I expect to see the plays if we're here that long. Both of them. I may make John let us stay on even if his work is done."

Kimberley said, gesturing at the town in general, "This is the place to see Shakespeare's plays, in his own town. And the summer festival is the best time of year to come."

As they entered the Holy Trinity Church, Penny saw the Shakespeare monument, a lifelike bust, affixed to the far wall at eye level.

She exclaimed, "There he is!" and hurried toward it.

Reaching the monument ahead of them, she eagerly read the inscription just beneath the bust. She said the last words aloud to the others who stood beside her—

"*. . . all that he hath writ leaves living art but page to serve his wit.*"

Then she read the ending words of the four lines of epitaph etched on the gravestone set into the brick floor immediately below the bust.

"*Cursed be he who moves my bones.*"

Penny and the others laughed aloud, then realized they were in the church, and stifled it. "That's quite an epitaph," Penny said. "Very Shakespearian."

"It's legendary, maybe even true," Anne Burghe said, "that the old bard wrote those four lines himself. He had a sense of humor, you know, and even his plays show it."

Penny could tell Anne was drawing upon her tourist spiel. She enjoyed seeing the sights, and it made her more eager to see the plays.

They lingered awhile, Penny reluctant to tear herself away from the monument, but finally moved on to see other sights. Anne Burghe took them past Mary Arden's house, the home of Shakespeare's mother of that maiden name, then on to the home which was Shakespeare's birthplace.

Penny, herself five feet, eight inches, remarked about the height of the interior doorways as they toured the house. "The people of that day weren't very tall," she remarked.

Anne smiled. "We've all grown in four hundred years."

Penny marveled at the timber-framed walls of the kitchen, raftered ceilings, brick and stone fireplace, and broken stone floor, and the period pieces in the living room. In a bedroom, she admired the seventeenth-century cradle, carved ornately of dark wood, and the quaint bedstead. She enjoyed seeing a prime example of the architecture of the fifteenth and six-teenth centuries, with the half-timber framing effect.

"I could live in a house like this," Penny said to Anne. She laughed, adding, "I know you've seen it a thousand times, but I can't help commenting."

"I never get tired of showing these historic things to people. My ancestors and family lived in Stratford, I was born here, I've lived here all my life, and I'm proud of it all."

Nearing one p.m., when Penny said she was becoming "a bit breathless from the walk," they stopped for lunch at a quaint tea shop, enjoying salads, sandwiches, and tea. "This is my treat," Kimberley said. "My husband said to be firm on that point."

After lunch, they continued their walking tour. "There's town hall," Kimberley Aylmer said as they came back across High Street toward the Inn. "My husband spends a lot of time there."

They reached the Inn soon, and Penny looked up at the window of their room. "John may be there by now. I enjoyed the tour."

Anne asked, "Would you like to see more tomorrow?"

"That would be nice. About noon?"

Anne nodded, and Kimberley Aylmer said, "We'll both be here. Consider me your assistant tour guide."

Anne said, "You liked the Shakespeare birthplace. Tomorrow we'll see the Anne Hathaway Cottage. It's a bit farther away, so we'll take a car there."

"I'll supply the car," Kimberley said.

Penny hurried into the lobby and up the stairs to their suite, anxious to see her husband and learn what he had found out and whether they'd stay the week, for both plays.

Chapter Four

Stratford, Monday Evening, June 23

John Barrymore's spirits brightened again as the motorcar drove into Stratford, across the small town, and up Scholar's Lane which became Chapel Lane and stopped in front of the Anne Hathaway Inn. He peered out the window at the Inn, saying, "Quaint," and waited for the driver to open the door. His valet, Brandon, jumped out the other door and began dealing with the baggage.

Barrymore descended from the vehicle, stretched his legs and arms, and strode up to the door of the Inn. He turned and looked back out over the town with a twinkle in his eye. "Not New York, is it Brandon?"

"No sir."

"But I like it. I can relax here, Brandon. I can feel it in the air already. Not as many bright lights as on Broadway—but I don't mind that. In fact, it's bad luck to notice the lights too much before your performance." He thought of the superstitions he and Lionel had shared ever since they took to the stage.

At the registration desk, the clerk said, "Oh, Mr. Barrymore, I've been told to call Mr. Flint, director of our plays, as soon as you arrived."

"Get us into our rooms, first, old man, and then call him. I want to change after the long day of driving. Some of the roads we were on were nothing more than dirt."

"Yes sir. The bellman will see you to your suite."

The entourage headed up the stairs, the bellman in the front loaded down with suitcases, followed by Brandon, car-

38

rying the remainder of the cases, and Barrymore with his light coat slung over his arm and his hat in hand. He glanced at his watch as they walked—five p.m. Was there time to see the theater, meet the ensemble cast, get any rehearsing in tonight? The Thursday night opening of *Macbeth* was just about seventy-two hours away.

On the second floor, they proceeded past a number of other room and suite doors to the end of the corridor and the choice corner suite Flint had reserved for them. When the bellman opened it, the three entered and Barrymore swiftly walked through it. He was not disappointed. A huge master bedroom and private bath, a secondary servant's room and smaller bath, a giant sitting room with fireplace and window looking in two directions up and down the lane.

On the large table in front of a plush sofa sat a bowl of fruit, a bottle of champagne already chilling in an ice bucket, and fresh flowers.

"Nice, very nice. Not home—not my own hideaway—but I can stand it for a week. Take care of the man, Brandon, and begin unpacking. I'll shave and clean up and change before Flint arrives." He consulted his watch again. "If there's a call from Flint, tell him he can come about six. And open the champagne."

Barrymore stepped into the bedroom-sized bathroom and over to the mirror. He studied his face, looking this way and that, inspecting his profile, and ample wavy hair. It was a vanity—he knew that. But he also knew his career depended upon his looks. *"Matinee idol,"* they called him, and he had to live up to it. Here, in the old world, he wondered whether the women would receive him with swoons, whether the costumes would be up to his standards, whether he could master two Shakespeare plays in one week, never having done Shakespeare at all before. His doubts and concerns were building, but he knew a cure for that.

"Bring that champagne in here, Brandon," he called. He turned on the water to run a bath, glad to see the steam rising soon from the water. A bath and a bottle. A good way to start the new experience.

As he sat in the tub sipping from his glass, he began to relish the thought of this adventure, as to which he had harbored some reservations in America. Now here, he saw the great possibilities. And if he could meet a handsome local woman, maybe one of the actresses, so much the better. It would enhance the pleasure of the trip.

Divorced from his first wife, Katherine, for a year and a half now, and not ready yet for a second, he was what some euphemistically, or perhaps realistically, for him, called "in between." Barrymore liked to think of the time as being space available for new adventures. Adventures worthy of the bawdy bard himself.

At six p.m. exactly, John Barrymore heard the rap on his hotel door and nodded at Brandon to attend to it. The valet admitted two men who stepped forward past Brandon to Barrymore, who had dressed casually for the evening with brown trousers, a tweed jacket, and a multi-colored scarf about his neck.

"Rex Flint," he said, "director of all the plays, Mr. Barrymore. So glad to meet you. A great pleasure."

Barrymore shook hands vigorously with the director. "My pleasure, too, sir," he said, but glanced sidelong at the other man standing patiently to one side. "And I'm sure you'll introduce me to . . . ?"

"Yes, yes—meet Professor John Darnell. A visitor to Stratford, but with a rather special purpose. John, meet John Barrymore."

"Always pleased to meet anyone named John," Barrymore said.

"We admire your acting from afar. My wife, who's from America, has been telling me about your acting family."

Barrymore laughed. "Yes, the addiction runs in the family. My sister Ethel and Lionel are in the racket, too." He frowned—never quite offstage when expressing his curiosity or dramatic interest—and said, "But you're here with a special purpose?" He looked from Darnell to Flint. "I expect you'll tell me about it."

Flint broke in, "That's why I brought him along. I thought we could explain that here in your rooms."

"Hmmm. Sounds mysterious. Brandon, let's kill that bottle of champagne, just about enough for three more glasses, I think."

The valet, who had been standing against the wall some distance away, crossed to the table and removed the champagne bottle from the ice bucket. In moments, he was passing around the glasses on a tray, after the three men had taken seats.

Barrymore held his glass up, saying, "To Shakespeare."

The others nodded and sipped their champagne.

Flint cleared his throat—a sign, Barrymore thought, of some nervousness—but spoke in a calm voice. "The whole of it is that we've had some, ah, quite mysterious events in town. Nothing to be concerned about, of course, but you should know of them."

Barrymore sipped his drink without comment. A dramatic pause was not unknown to him. He'd wait.

"The fact is," Flint went on, "that two people have complained of seeing ghosts in Stratford."

"Ghosts?" Barrymore's initial smile turned into a frown as possible implications quickly crossed his mind. "I'm waiting to hear."

Flint described the two events in as much detail as he had garnered himself, second or third hand, from the witness reports.

He looked expectantly at the actor.

"Twice in the past week? And what effect will this have on attendance? I'm not sure I like competing with a ghost."

"That's where Professor Darnell comes in. He's what I would call a 'ghost-chaser.' "

Darnell returned Barrymore's gaze which now fell on him. "I debunk all sorts of supernatural or paranormal phenomena. The world seems to be fascinated with it more than ever these days."

"These days? You mean since the war?" Barrymore nodded. "Yes, I can understand that. After a war, it's left to the artist to keep its sordid memory, to help the world go through the grieving process, the numbness, the great loss . . ."

"A terrible loss here," Darnell said. "Millions of men."

Barrymore went on with his short monologue. ". . . and Shakespeare has become a universal language, a unifying common denominator for all classic expression, whether in his plays or poetry. Someday, I'll do Hamlet in London . . ." He paused. "But getting back to your ghosts," he said, turning to Darnell, "do you have any kind of explanation?"

Darnell shook his head. "Not yet. I arrived last night."

"Will audiences be frightened away?"

"It's unlikely," Darnell said, "unless something else occurs. These sightings were tame enough. No one made any contact and no one was hurt."

"Hurt—by a ghost?" Barrymore raised his eyebrows.

"Correct, doubly impossible. The point is that these were not ghosts at all, that someone very human is simply passing himself off as a spirit. I've seen this before, and it sometimes leads to violence, and death, in our real world."

"Couldn't it just be some trouble-maker?"

"Perhaps. I tend to think so. We'll find out."

"You're an investigator?"

"Yes."

"Then let's hope you do find the answer."

Flint spoke up. "There is, well, one more small thing." John Barrymore listened intently as Flint told of the drowning of the cats.

"I know that line, *'drown cats,'* " Barrymore said. "Iago speaks it early in the play. So—it's a reference to Othello."

"Yes. The play that was put on the night before."

Barrymore frowned. "Did your, ah, ghost, drown them?"

"I think not," Darnell said. "Just a guess at this point, but the act of killing animals to make a point involves a deeper sense of mischief than merely dressing up like a ghost."

"Shakespeare likes ghosts," Barrymore mused. "There's one in *Macbeth*, one in *Hamlet*, many in *Richard*."

"I imagine you'd like to see the theater." Flint looked at him.

"You're reading my mind. I'm anxious to walk the stage."

"Of course," Flint said.

"Please come along, Professor," Barrymore said with a smile. "Just in case we see any more ghosts along the way."

Penny felt at loose ends. John Darnell and she had enjoyed tea in their rooms, and they'd spent some time together that afternoon. But when he received the call from Flint, he explained his need to accompany the director to meet Barrymore, and promised to return in time for dinner.

Six-thirty now, and John wouldn't be back for an hour or two, and she wouldn't see the mayor's wife or the tour guide until noon the next day. She'd looked through all the local travel and tourist brochures and magazines, and wanted something to do. At dusk now, the town's decorative streetlamps had come on, and some shops closed. She looked out the window, watching tourists walking the streets, stopping in at shops that remained open, planning dinner, soaking up the town's atmosphere by night.

In the utter silence of their room, Penny jumped at the sudden loud knock at her door, but she opened it with anticipation.

Anne Burghe stood in the hall at the doorway. "Penny? Are you busy?" She looked into the room, first one direction, then the other. "Is your husband here?"

Penny smiled. "No, to both. I'm quite alone. Would you like to come in?"

Anne Burghe nodded and entered hesitantly. "I had hoped your husband might be here, but . . ."

"I'm glad you came. Maybe I can return some of your hospitality. Would you like some sherry? John ordered up a bottle. I don't drink alcohol just now, you know," she said, "but I'd like to serve you some."

Anne had settled herself in a chair and answered, "Yes, please. I'd enjoy it."

Penny filled a small, delicate glass with the amber sherry and handed it to her visitor. "I think there's something you want to tell us, or ask us, isn't there, Anne." She could see concern in the woman's face.

Anne Burghe took a swallow of sherry. "I don't know if you were told this, but I was the person who saw the ghost Saturday night. That was the second time, and I think it led to the mayor calling your husband. He told me he had to do something."

"I didn't know you'd seen it. Did it startle you?"

Anne shivered. "I can still remember the feeling, when I talk of it."

"Is that why you're here, now?"

"I . . . I did want to ask him, well, could there really be such a thing? A ghost?"

Penny laughed lightly. "I think I can safely answer that for John. He has absolutely no belief in anything supernatural. Not in apparitions, ghosts, séances, jinxes. Maybe you don't know this, but he debunks these things. It's what he does. He proves they *aren't* true."

"Then what is it, or who is it?"

"That's why John's here. He'll find out. He hasn't failed yet, since I've known him. Seven years now."

Anne frowned. "I'm glad to hear that. But there's more." She paused and sipped from her glass. "I have a daughter. She's fourteen, and away at private school. I couldn't afford that, of course. My father set up a trust fund for her before he died a few years ago. Wanted her to have the best education."

"Do you see her often?"

"All holidays. And she'll be home for the summer soon. The thing is—I want the best for her, want to be able to provide for her."

Penny thought of her own coming duties as a mother, and could appreciate Anne's feelings. "I know what you mean."

"I have some things that have come down to me from my family, in my home. I don't know their value, and I thought Professor Darnell, coming from London, might be able to refer me to someone to give me some advice. I want to do what I can for Anna Maria. Of course, I know your husband's busy right now—but before he leaves Stratford . . . ?"

"Of course. I'll tell John about it. He'll be glad to help any way he can."

"Thanks. I'll talk with him in a few days."

"I'm sure we'll be here through Saturday night. I won't let him leave before I see Barrymore play Hamlet!"

Chapter Five

Monday Evening, June 23

Rex Flint led the way briskly along Chapel Lane toward the River Avon and the Shakespeare Memorial Theater. As they reached the theater, Barrymore interrupted a story he'd been telling Darnell about his brother and sister, Lionel and Ethel, stopped abruptly, and stared at the theater.

"It's beautiful! I love it!" He slowly walked around the rotunda-like circular building at the forefront of the Victorian Gothic structure. "How many does it hold?"

"Audience?" Flint smiled. "Thinking of the attendance already? Well, about eight hundred. Plus standing room."

Barrymore strutted back and forth, admiring the towers and spires. "They'll stand to see me, I think." He turned to Darnell. "Unless they're preoccupied with the town ghost."

"I'm sure they'd rather see you."

Flint said, "Let's go inside." As they proceeded, he explained that the theater was almost forty years old, opened in 1879. "A local brewer helped build it, donating the two acres of grounds," he said, "and his family still contributes."

The night watchman greeted them at the stage door entrance, the time now being after seven p.m., and Flint introduced the uniformed man, Onslow Skelton, to them. The watchman rose from his desk and limped over to them, shaking hands with the newcomers.

"I used to be an actor myself, Mr. Barrymore," Skelton said. "Fell into the orchestra pit, if you can believe that. Got this bad leg. Laid up for a long time. After that, well, I just gave up acting. Now, my daughter—I have plans for her. She'll be a great actress if she listens to me. Oh, I shouldn't ramble on."

Barrymore said, "No, it's a pleasure to meet you, Onslow. What parts did you play?"

"Falstaff. Lear. Macduff. Many others."

"I hope you'll be able to see my performances this week."

Skelton nodded. "I'll be watching in the wings. Both nights."

Flint and Barrymore walked on ahead into the wings of the stage area. Darnell held back, saying, "I'll be along soon."

He heard Flint's remark, ". . . doing his investigating," as the two walked away.

The watchman looked expectantly at Darnell, who said, "You've heard about the ghost sightings, Onslow?"

"Yes sir. Constable Clive told me about them. Ed said the tourist was agitated. Anne Burghe, a tour guide, you know, was disturbed about it too. So it was real enough."

Darnell nodded. "In the theater here there was that event, the curtain weight accident. Were you here when it fell?"

Skelton shook his head. "It was during the day. I work seven p.m. to five a.m." He smiled. "Nothing ever happens at night anymore, but at one time costumes had been stolen. I'm lonely at night, but I'm not complainin'. I need the work."

"Did you examine the curtain weight, the rope?"

"I did, sir." He lowered his voice. "The rope was frayed. And I've been around the stage enough to know these things can happen. But I also thought it might have been helped along, cut part way." He paused. "Still, I don't want to spread rumors."

"You're saying it might not have been an accident."

"The stage director, Danny Marek, could tell you more."

Darnell saw the watchman had said all he would, thanked him, and caught up with Barrymore and Flint on the stage.

Barrymore paced back and forth staring out at the sea of empty seats. "I like it," he said. Then in a louder voice, one he would use to project farther and more loudly during a stage performance, he declaimed, *"I have done the state some service, and they know it."*

He was pleased to hear his words reverberate around the theater. He turned to Flint, "Good. I think they'll hear me all right."

Flint nodded, eyes sparkling.

Barrymore went on, "I need to train my voice more, I know that, for Shakespeare. When I return to New York and finish up with *The Jest*, I'll do that. It could run another six months."

"You'll do Shakespeare in America?" Darnell asked.

"Yes. My goal is *Hamlet*, but I won't start with that, although this is important here. To get my taste of it and *Macbeth*. Maybe I'll do *Richard the Third* there first." He nodded to himself. "Yes—for practice."

Flint said, "Your voice will be fine here. We'll have some good rehearsals tomorrow. And we'll have three full days and two nights before the first play opens. It'll be grueling, John. Meeting actors and actresses, rehearsing it all."

Barrymore spread his arms wide and strode across the stage and back, saying, *"All the world's a stage."* He stopped in front of Flint, faced him, and rested both hands dramatically on the other's shoulders. "Don't worry, Rex. I've got all my lines down pat. I've been rehearsing on my own with some friends in New York for months." He smiled. "Even in bed."

After their tour of the theater, and with none of the cast

around at that hour, they returned to the Inn. Flint said good-night to them at the door, but arranged to see Barrymore the next morning at the theater promptly at nine to begin re-hearsals. "Latimer will be there, and all the cast and supporting actors and crew. I want them all to meet you and we need to get started."

Barrymore agreed with that, and he and Darnell entered the lobby. "Let's have dinner together," Barrymore said. "The mayor said something about being here tonight. Your wife, of course."

Darnell nodded. "We'd enjoy it. Eight p.m.? Down-stairs?"

They walked up the stairs together, Darnell stopping at his door and nodding at Barrymore who continued on to his corner suite at the end of the hall. As Darnell entered, he saw Penny clearing away glasses and a sherry bottle.

"Hello, dear. You had a caller?"

Penny told him about Anne Burghe's visit, and her wish to speak with him about items in her home, old family posses-sions. "She has something on her mind," Penny said, frowning. "Of course, she saw that ghost-thing on Saturday night. Enough to bother anyone."

"I don't know much about antiques, but I can recommend a dealer."

"I think that's what she wants."

When he told her of dining with John Barrymore, her mood brightened, and she said, "I must change."

Darnell shaved again as she selected a different dress. When they were ready he said, "Let's go on down. If they're not there yet, we'll sit in the lounge."

But as they descended the staircase, he saw Barrymore standing in the lounge, flanked by Mayor Aylmer and his wife.

"We have a table ready in the corner by the window," the mayor said, "where we can talk in comfort." He led the way across the lobby and into the restaurant. In minutes they were seated at their table. The waiter filled their water glasses, laid their napkins in their laps, and presented the menus. He handed a wine menu to Barrymore and said he'd return soon.

When the waiter returned, Barrymore and the mayor discussed wine, reached agreement on a white and a red and ordered both, and all ordered their food. Darnell knew that each in their own way wanted to ask the actor questions about America, the stage, and what he expected in Stratford.

As the waiter walked away, Penny asked the first one. "Has America changed much in the past seven years? I haven't seen New York since 1912."

Barrymore nodded. "It's changed, yes, and for the better I'd say. Not as many horses in New York City, being replaced by cars and buses you know. The lighting is better in the streets. The war's over. It was a strain on President Wilson, of course. But people are optimistic. A new election coming. Yes, it's better. Everyone's ready to roar ahead into the nineteen twenties."

Kimberley Aylmer smiled and spoke tentatively. "I want to ask whether you like acting, but I know you do. Maybe I should ask what you *like* about it."

John Barrymore laughed. "I guess I like it. Love might be a better word, although sometimes it's love and hate mixed. I had my first role, not a big one, on stage when I was barely eighteen, first good roles at twenty-one. Over thirty roles on the stage, with a dozen motion pictures thrown in. And not yet forty years old. I've got some plans to do Shakespeare in America, that's why I wanted this experience here. It'll be a learning time for me."

"You've not done Shakespeare before?" she asked.

"Only in my rehearsals the past few months in America. Never on the stage. The whole idea is a mystery. Just think about it—we speak words written over three hundred years ago by a man who is himself a mystery. We know so little about him. And we try to recreate the emotions on stage that he wanted us to show when he wrote the words, emotions he may have shown himself when he acted in plays, or suggested to actors how to speak his words."

" 'Trippingly on the tongue,' " Darnell said.

"Exactly." He smiled. "And I hope I don't trip over my tongue getting the words out."

The others laughed, and sat back as the waiter served wine to all but Penny and their salads or soups. They ate quietly for a minute or two until Barrymore spoke.

"Lionel prefers Macbeth. He can have him. It's Hamlet, the Prince of Denmark, who captivates me. This will be excellent practice, a good preparation for me."

Aylmer said, "You go from Macbeth to Hamlet two nights apart."

"Quite a transition, yes. But I think the audience will be forgiving of me. I know the lines well. It's getting into the right frame of mind, putting yourself into the character before the play opens—that's the hard part."

"How do you do that?" Penny asked.

"How to become someone else for three hours? The costumes help. I try facial expressions. I look for the emotions in it. I go over the words of Shakespeare, Macbeth's or Hamlet's lines—and I love the lines." He smiled. "I can't speak one of the best lines in *Hamlet* because it's said about him after he dies at the end, as an epitaph—*"Good night, sweet prince—and flights of angels sing thee to thy rest."*

He motioned to the waiter to come fill the four wine glasses again. Food courses were placed before them.

52

John Barrymore smiled at Penny. "You're going to have a little Prince of your own."

She laughed lightly. "Prince, maybe—or Princess. We'll love either one."

"I'm sensing it could be a sweet Prince, but maybe I've got Hamlet on my mind." He turned to Darnell. "No ghost tonight, eh, John? Did we scare him away?"

At the word "ghost," Darnell looked about the room to see if anyone was listening to their conversation. It seemed many curious eyes were on Barrymore or Penny from time to time, but their table was distant enough so that most of their words could not be overheard. He saw that the mayor had looked around also, and knew he was sensitive to the ghost issue.

Satisfied, Darnell answered Barrymore in a low voice. "I don't think we've seen the last of him. He'll only come at night, of course. Maybe later tonight, or tomorrow night. I rather expect one more appearance before your plays begin on Thursday."

"Then is it predictable, that he'll come again?" Kimberley Aylmer looked at Darnell with some concern.

"Not at all. We need to be on our watch, because I think the things that have happened so far are only a bizarre prelude of some sort. And I don't believe our perpetrator is done with his mischief yet. But I just hope his actions stay at this mischievous level and don't lead into something more dangerous—or more deadly."

Chapter Six

Tuesday Morning, June 24

The morning broke brightly in Stratford and the Anne Hathaway Inn seemed transformed on the new day with a bustle of activity. When Darnell and Penny went down for breakfast, they saw tourists arriving in bunches now, knowing they all wanted to settle into their rooms in anticipation of the plays later that week and meanwhile to see the town. After registering and quick breakfasts, groups in twos and fours, some with children, some older couples, streamed onto the streets of Stratford-upon-Avon.

Among them, after finishing their early breakfast, Darnell saw John Barrymore exit by the front door just before nine and, outside, turn toward the Memorial Theater. "His rehearsals," Darnell told Penny. "I want to see them, too."

"You go on John," Penny said. "I have some things to do in the room, then I'll prowl around the hotel shops until noon."

"Anne Burghe's coming?"

"And the mayor's wife. Kimberley's so nice." She smiled. "Motherly, you know."

He smiled. "It's a chance to observe and learn."

They returned to their rooms, and, after he made sure Penny was comfortably ensconced there, Darnell quickly pulled on a casual jacket and headed down the stairs, across the lobby, and toward the theater. When he arrived, he found the stage and wings hummed with conversation and people moving back and forth.

Rex Flint, standing with the producer, Richard Latimer, and John Barrymore, saw Darnell enter and called him over. "Just in time. I'm going to introduce Mr. Barrymore to everyone. I know Richard wants to talk with you later, and I'll see that you meet the key actors and actresses then for the two plays."

Darnell nodded, and stepped aside as Flint put a hand on Barrymore's shoulder and called out to everyone, "Quiet, please."

The buzz of talk subsided and all eyes were on Flint and Barrymore. Darnell stood discreetly farther away from the three men and blended into one of the groups of actors and hands who were giving Flint their attention and took no notice of Darnell.

Flint began, "My good casts, my actors, my great stage directors and decorators and stagehands, my dear friends . . . allow me to introduce the famous American stage and screen actor, Mr. John Barrymore. He is currently on summer hiatus from his play, *The Jest*, and is a prominent member of the most illustrious acting family in the United States, the Barrymores, in which Ethel and Lionel Barrymore, his sister and brother, are also very active and popular on the stage. Here is Mr. John Barrymore."

The assembled people broke into applause which lasted for a full minute, until Flint held up a hand. Another semi-hush fell over the crowd, although whispers among those who stood looking at them could be heard flickering around the room.

"Mr. Barrymore, as you know, will star in *Macbeth* Thursday night and *Hamlet* Saturday night. We need to begin intensive rehearsals day and night. He needs to get to know you, you need to learn about him, and you all need to get your lines down. As the stage and costuming people complete their work, the sets and the costumes, you'll all work together and polish your lines. I know you've learned them over the past few months, as has Mr. Barrymore. We'll have a full dress rehearsal of *Macbeth* Wednesday night—I know, that's tomorrow—last minute run-throughs and costumes, and the play Thursday night. Then we go right into rehearsing *Hamlet* Friday, and we'll have that all that day, a dress rehearsal Friday evening, and polishing Saturday."

He listened to the undertone of conversation buzzing for a moment, then added, "I know that's a lot of switching of moods and lines and some hard work. Are you game for it?"

Loud applause and words of commitment followed his last words. He beamed at Barrymore and the crowd.

"Now, I want everyone to meet Mr. Barrymore personally. We'll start with the entire casts of *Macbeth* and *Hamlet*, first, to just come up here to us so you can say hello and get acquainted a bit. Then everyone else, no particular order."

Darnell watched as the actors and actresses and hands filed up to Flint and Barrymore. As he watched them approach the two men and speak and smile and shake hands, he thought . . . *One or more of them may have drowned those cats, worn a ghost costume, fixed that heavy weight to come down and almost kill the actress, Portia Regan. But right now—they're all smiling.*

John Barrymore enjoyed the proceedings. As each person came up to him, Flint or Latimer announced the name, Barrymore took the hand outstretched, or offered his own, wanting not only to know the people but to make them feel comfortable. He knew he'd not remember all the names, but as he met some of the women, he knew he would not forget theirs. He was better at women's names.

The names and faces flowed before him. Many minor

stage hands, character actors, bit players, whose names he'd have to learn over the week but might never fix in his mind. And, most importantly, the primary actors and actresses who would loom large in the plays. He had no trouble knowing who they were because Rex Flint would emphasize their importance by subtle nuances in the way he would introduce them, as well as his pointing out what parts they'd take in the plays when he introduced them by their real names. Barrymore liked that, and also appreciated Flint's skill in doing so.

Out of the corner of his eye, he noticed John Darnell observing the people as they were being introduced, and realized the professor was doing a bit of quiet note-taking and memorization of his own in his investigation. A thought flashed in Barrymore's mind—*could one of these men be the ghost?*

The pleasant voice of the woman in front of him, holding out her hand toward him, brought him back. Flint had announced her name, Felicia Baron, and indicated she had key roles in *Macbeth* and *Hamlet*. He looked into her eyes as she spoke, and thought he saw more there than was revealed in her formal words.

"Mr. Barrymore," she said in a crisp, cultured voice, "I'm so glad to meet you. And I'll be looking forward to acting in *Macbeth* and *Hamlet* with you. I'm Lady Macbeth and Ophelia. These will be some of the most exciting nights of my life."

"Dear lady, the pleasure will be all mine, I assure you. I want to talk with you more about your roles, when we have time."

"Any time." Her clear green eyes teased and she tossed back her bountiful head of long, light brown hair as she moved on.

Next in the line came an eager young man, an actor in his twenties, Barrymore guessed, and found himself to be right.

Flint introduced him, saying, "This is Stanford Vance. He'll be in both plays this week."

Barrymore smiled at the young actor, recalling how he felt at twenty-one in his first significant roles. "You've certainly got the name for an actor. Is that a stage name?"

"No, sir, I was born with it. I—well, I want to learn from you while you're here. It's an opportunity I never thought I'd have."

"It's a good way to learn," Barrymore said, with a twinkle in his eye. "Watching older actors."

"Oh, I didn't mean . . ."

"It's all right. I tease myself sometimes. Actually, at thirty-seven, I feel I'm just getting started. If you want advice, keep taking roles when they're offered. Don't be too particular. Act, act, and act some more. Get a lot of plays and roles under your belt."

"Yes, sir." Vance moved away, making room for the next.

An actor at the other extreme, Barrymore thought, showing gray and white hair about the ears but little on top. He faced Barrymore and stuck out a gnarled hand. "Montague Bourne," he said. "What you might call a character actor, Mr. Barrymore. Definitely a character. I've been acting here for a dozen or more years, and before that on the London stage."

"You're never too old to act. Plenty of good roles."

"I'm going to talk Rex into letting me do Lear next year."

"Good, very good."

Others moved through the long line—stage hands, ushers. Judith Shandy, a thirtyish actress with flaming red hair. A tall, muscular actor with long, wavy, actor-type hair—Avery Ainsley. The names and faces swam before his eyes.

After Ainsley stepped by, Flint whispered to Barrymore that the actor would have starred in *Macbeth* and *Hamlet* this summer had John Barrymore not come. "But he'll be Banquo and Horatio."

"I hope he's not resentful," Barrymore said.

Flint said, unsmiling, "He has his career to think about."

Willa Skelton, the night watchman's daughter, talked with Barrymore, saying, "My father said I should meet you. He wants me to be an actress. What do you think?"

Barrymore inspected her willowy frame and dark brown hair. "Looks and voice. That's what's important. You'd have a good head start in both respects. Listen to your father."

He met many others. Reid Perkins, a young actor . . . Danny Marek, stage director working under Flint . . . Portia Regan, a black-haired beauty with deep blue eyes and high cheekbones. As she stood talking with Barrymore, her gaze drifted over to Rex Flint often and Barrymore wondered what was in her mind. A better role? That was the usual ambition. And other actors and actresses, some cast in the three plays. Lily Camden, a gray-haired plump woman . . . Philip Dennis, a brash, sandy-haired outspoken man . . . Karen Nettles, gray-haired and slim. And there seemed to be an international contingent—Barry McClintoch, with a Scotch accent . . . Erik Berg, with a touch of German accent . . . Pierre Gaston with a bit of a French one . . . James O'Bairne, either Irish or Scotch, or both. And other interesting women such as Erin Daly, easy on the eyes, swishing away with a flourish after their meeting. But his eyes kept drifting over to Felicia Baron, where she sat, watching him.

He wearied, but stayed on until he had met the casts for both plays, other actors and actresses, and all the stage hands.

"Whew," he said to Flint and Latimer, as the last walked away, all of them going about their duties in their need to be ready for rehearsals soon that morning. "I could stand a cup of strong coffee."

Flint said to Latimer, "What do you say, Richard? Shall we walk down to your office with Mr. Barrymore and Professor Darnell? Get coffee on the way?"

The producer said, "Let's do it. That'll allow me to ask the professor some questions. You lead the way. I'll stay back with him so we can talk."

Flint told Danny Marek he and Barrymore would be back in half an hour to begin rehearsals on *Macbeth*, and to prepare seating on stage and sufficient scripts for all. The four men walked up the aisle and out the door.

Outside, John Barrymore took a deep breath and said, "Clean Stratford air! That'll help clear my mind. I may have had one too many last night, celebrating my arrival. Let's make the walk brisk, Rex. I've about shaken my hand off meeting everyone. I need to exercise some other parts of my body, stretch my legs."

Flint and Barrymore walked a few steps ahead, spiritedly discussing the rehearsal program. Richard Latimer and Darnell lagged behind.

Latimer rubbed a hand over his balding head, rearranging the remaining black hair. He began directly, saying, "That falling curtain weight last Saturday was no accident. I'm convinced of it. I know the evidence isn't there, and there's nothing we can tell our constable that would trigger an investigation. It's ambiguous. But with the cat incident and two ghost appearances . . . well, what do you make of it? That's what I want to know."

Between the lines of what Latimer said, Darnell could see the man was disturbed by the prospect of worse things coming. His entire summer festival might be at stake. "I won't make light of it," Darnell said, "because many people regard ghosts seriously. The theory is, ghosts perpetuate something disastrous that happened at a location, and continue to inhabit the place. I've found supposed sightings a prelude to something more significant. The cats tie in to Iago's line in *Othello*, a cruel hint of trouble." He paused. "But the so-called accident of the weight falling is what bothers me most. Your watchman said the old rope was evidently frayed, but could have been helped along with a knife. Did the constable inspect it?"

"Yes. You should speak with him. I'll take you to his office later. It's on the next street over, a few blocks away. But I can tell you he said the evidence was inconclusive, but there had been a possible attempt to hurt someone."

"That someone being Portia Regan?"

"Yes."

They passed gift shops, restaurants, a bookstore announcing the sale of new and rare collectibles, a photography shop, everything a tourist might want, including the coffee shop within the block.

"Before we get there," Darnell said, "I don't want to alarm Mr. Barrymore about this without anything concrete. But I'd like to see Miss Regan. The fact that she was almost struck by a deadly object could mean she was a *specific* target, that someone wanted to hurt *her* in particular. If so, the question is why."

"I didn't think of that."

"After I quiz the constable, I'll look her up at the theater—with your permission. And with everything kept very confidential."

"Of course." Latimer sighed.

The four entered the coffee shop, took a table and ordered.

Fifteen minutes later, after discussing rehearsals for the

day, Flint said, "We need to get back. There's a lot to do."

The director and Barrymore headed back to the theater while Darnell walked with Latimer over one street and then up several blocks, away from the center of town and the bulk of the tourist traffic, to an unobtrusive small wooden building bearing a door sign saying, "Constable." The rear of the building with barred windows obviously constituted a small jail. Darnell suspected that part of the facility received little use in this village.

Constable Edgar Clive rose from his chair behind the weathered desk and extended a hand to Richard Latimer. He eyed Darnell sidelong. "You're Professor Darnell," he said, "the ghost hunter." He put his hand out to him next.

Darnell smiled. "I go by various names. Depends on what people call me. I investigate the unusual."

He and Latimer sat in the two straight-backed chairs that faced Constable Clive's desk. A young deputy sat at a small side desk. The constable returned to his swivel chair that barely accommodated his bulk of what Darnell thought could be sixteen stone—at least two hundred twenty-five pounds—more than the man needed for his height of about five feet eight, but offering no doubt an appearance of solidity to the townspeople. Clive's gray hair at his temples enhanced his aura of authority.

"I don't get cases like this situation," Clive said. "Once in a while a tourist will get out of hand, too much to drink, you know. Maybe a dispute about shoplifting. Nothing like ghosts. Or dead cats." He looked expectantly at Darnell.

"I hope I can help. I'd like to ask you about what you know about all this. I've been told you've had contact with people who reported all four occurrences."

"That's true. What would you like to know?"

"Let's take them one by one. The drowned cats."

Clive nodded. "A boy came to me, was fishing although not supposed to. Brave of him to tell me. Anyway, three cats in the potato sack. One black, the others not. Strays, I'd say."

"No indication of who did it, I suppose, or why."

"None."

"The ghosts . . ."

"A tourist came to my office Thursday morning after he saw it late Wednesday night after seeing a play and visiting a pub. I wondered if it was the ale, but he said no, he was leaving town then, and felt a duty to report it. He seemed serious enough."

"And the second sighting, Saturday night by Anne Burghe?"

"I'd trust her word anywhere. She saw it, all right. What it was, she doesn't know. A man dressed up like a ghost, with a stage costume, pasty white face, she said. A description very similar to the one the tourist gave me."

"And one more thing, perhaps most important—the accident at the theater last week."

He nodded. "Yes. Six inches farther over the weight would have crushed Portia. She was almost scared to death as it was, so to speak."

"You consider it an accident?"

"I can't call it anything else, although the old, frayed rope could have been helped along. With a knife."

"Is there anything else that might make you think it was, say, an intentional act?"

He frowned. "No. I talked with Portia and Danny—at the theater. Nothing came of it. But . . ."

"But you're not sure."

"Right. And, well, I am a bit worried. What if it happened again, and this time someone was really hurt—or killed?"

Chapter Seven

Tuesday Morning, June 24

The call came in to Penny's room about ten thirty, just as she returned from a tour of the shops on the ground floor of the Inn, wondering how she'd spend the next hour and a half until her tour companions arrived. She picked up the receiver and spoke into it.

The voice she heard was the familiar one of Kimberley Aylmer. "We thought we'd come a bit early, Penny, Anne and I. I decided you'd probably be moping around the room and could use some company."

"You must read minds. That would be wonderful. I was just trying to decide what to do until noon."

"Good. Then we'll be there at eleven. I'll be driving our family car and I'll pick Anne up on the way to you."

Eleven a.m. sharp, in the front of the Inn, became the plan and at that exact time Penny looked up Scholars Lane at the approaching vehicle and smiled as it pulled up in front of the Inn.

She stepped in and greeted them. "So, to Anne Hathaway's cottage?"

Anne Burghe nodded. "You liked Shakespeare's birthplace and you'll love this home. Sorry, it's not for rent."

They laughed, and Penny sat back to enjoy the sights as they proceeded through the town and down roads to the home about a mile away. When they arrived and walked up to it, joining groups of tourists who milled about, she admired the bountiful greenery about the grounds—the garden, the shrubs, trees, and bushes. "I love the brown picket fence, and that gate," she said, "and the stone-work and half-timber look and thatched roof. It's beautiful. It's much more than a mere cottage, though."

Anne nodded. "That's a bit deceiving, if you're expecting a small one or two room single-story place. It was originally a farmhouse. But it has the comfort of a cottage."

Inside they toured slowly, taking time to look closely at the ornate carved Elizabethan bedstead, cradle of matching wood, and other belongings of the Hathaway family that dated back, as part of the cottage did, to the fifteenth century.

Afterward, they repeated their experience of the day before, stopping at a different tea shop for lunch. Penny told Anne that Darnell would speak to her about her antiques before they left.

"Oh, it's not antiques, really. But I'll tell him about it when I see him."

They ordered food and tea and enjoyed the leisure time in the quaint shop.

"The families in Stratford date back a long time, don't they, with descendants here today?" Penny looked from one to the other.

"Yes," Anne said. "But they're not necessarily carrying on family traditions. They may be doing other things. And they may be only distantly related, with perhaps only the name itself a connection."

"None named Shakespeare, I'm guessing."

"That's right. His son died young and his two daughters married and took their husbands' names, Hall and Quiney."

"I'd like to stop at the theater and catch up with John. He'd be watching rehearsals by now, I think."

Kimberley said, "Missing your husband. I know. We'll drive you there and drop you off just as soon as we finish."

She smiled. "I'm sure Professor Darnell wants to see you too."

When Latimer and Darnell left the constable's office, the producer went to his office and said he'd return to the theater soon. Darnell took the opportunity for a casual stroll back through Stratford. As he walked along the streets of the town toward the River Avon and the Memorial Theater, amid the increasing throngs of tourists, he peered into shops in passing, stopping here and there to study displays in the windows. One shop, a bookstore, Blount's Books: New and Collectibles, intrigued him because of his enjoyment of history and old tomes.

He stepped inside to look about, finding it lined with shelves laden with books, some looking very old, possibly either expensively collectible or just not the sort of light reading a tourist would enjoy. Maybe he could find a good book about Shakespeare and about the town's history. Several customers moved about the store. He joined them and strolled through it.

He picked up a book here and there, glanced at those on shelves, and began to find his way around. A man, almost as tall as he but stockier, sporting an unruly crop of jet black hair, approached him and said, "Looking for anything in particular? Something on Shakespeare? I'm the owner." His white shirt, black trousers, vest, and bow tie constituted a uniform of sorts.

Darnell said, "Yes. Something rare, if you have it. I don't mean anything particularly valuable—just something a bit different, a good souvenir to relish."

"Ah, yes. Hmmm—I do have a few books that would fit that description. Come back here." He walked to a shelf behind the sales counter and reached up, taking down several volumes. "I keep them handy to browse through when days are slow." He laid them on the counter and invited Darnell to look at them.

As Darnell turned the pages slowly in one book and the next, he felt the gaze of the dark eyes of the owner on him.

"You're the professor, aren't you?" the man said at last.

Darnell looked up, surprised, wondering how his reputation had made it even into the depths of a local bookstore.

"Ye-es. But . . ."

"Anne told me about you. Anne Burghe." He laughed. "This is a small town. Word gets around."

"I'm just another tourist."

"Yes?" The man held out a hand. "Victor Blount."

Darnell shook it reluctantly. He didn't like this notoriety so early in the case. He hurriedly selected two of the books, saying, "I'll take these." He paid the prices indicated and left the shop. Outside he mumbled to himself, *"Small town."*

Darnell thought of the name, Blount, and realized where he'd seen it before, on a reproduction of a Shakespeare portrait from a printed folio of his plays. *Blount.* Interesting. The same family? He'd ask Anne Burghe. As he walked he seemed to feel the eyes of pedestrians on the back of his head. Had word about his coming gone so far? He turned around, feeling someone was following him, but saw no evidence of it. He shook his head.

He reached the river two blocks down from the theater and walked along the bank, observing the bridge, speculating as to the motive of a man who would drown cats in a potato sack. Not a ghostly act. All agreed on that. Approaching the theater, he saw a bustle of activity at the entrance. Rex Flint was helping two gray-haired women—in their seventies, he guessed—out of a car. One of them was missing a leg and walking with crutches. Flint led them to the front entrance just as John Barrymore stepped through the doorway and rushed forward to greet them.

"Sarah!" Barrymore said. "Sarah Bernhardt! What . . . ?"

Flint smiled. "My secret, John. Sarah wanted to come while you were here, so I put together roles for her and for Ellen. This is Ellen Terry, John. Ellen . . . John Barrymore."

"I'm overwhelmed. Small roles you say? For world-famous actresses. I can't imagine." Barrymore shook his head, but took the hands of both the women, first Bernhardt, then Terry. To Terry, he said, "I saw you once on the stage when I was a mere boy."

"Witches," Flint said. "They want to be witches. In *Macbeth*, of course."

Barrymore roared with laughter. "What a great idea! What a delight! The Divine Sarah and Ellen Terry as witches!"

Seeing Darnell approach, Flint introduced him quickly as Professor Darnell and said, "Let's get these women inside so they can rest after their journey from London." As they all walked slowly, Flint explained that he'd secured rooms for them on the ground floor of the Anne Hathaway Inn. "All my important people at the same location. And the ground floor, Sarah—easier for you to get in and out."

"Don't you worry." As if to prove it, she walked ahead of them, skillfully using her crutches. "They wanted to carry me in a litter chair, like they've been doing. No! Not here."

"Wait for us!" Flint said. "I believe you."

Inside, they took seats on sofas in the lobby and Barrymore and Sarah Bernhardt began a dialogue about the theater and past experiences that fascinated Darnell, but left him out of the exchange.

He turned to Ellen Terry and remarked, "I had occasion to work with George Bernard Shaw two years ago. You starred in a number of his plays, I know."

Ellen Terry nodded, saying, "Yes, several, and I enjoyed them. He should be a character in his own plays. Write himself in. There's no one like Bernard."

"He's said the same of you."

"I guess you'd call Sarah and me the grand old ladies of the stage. I don't really act anymore, but Sarah, she refuses to quit." She lowered her voice. "Even after she lost her leg. She sits down when she acts now."

"Are you talking about me?" Sarah demanded.

"I said, you'd make a good witch."

She sniffed. "That's not what I heard."

"Just relax, Sarah. Remember, it was your idea to come up here. Now enjoy it."

Rex Flint cleared his throat and said, "We're just begun rehearsals for *Macbeth*. Come down to the stage. I'll introduce you to the cast. You're just in time. We're beginning with the first act, and, of course, you'll be in it. You don't have to stay all day if you want to relax at the Inn. My car and driver will be in front, and he'll take you wherever you want to go."

Sarah said, "I want to hear Barrymore say his lines. Let's go up on the stage, get on with the rehearsals. Right, Ellen?"

"My idea exactly. We can relax tonight after dinner."

Unlike many stage stars, John Barrymore enjoyed the beginnings of rehearsals with the cast. It always involved some tedium, yes—hearing the same lines over and over—but it also put emphasis on getting the lines right, the nuances and shadings of the words. And it brought the people who would be on stage during the performance together for the first time. It was a chance to meet them, absent their costumes, see them as human beings before they took on the aura of their fictional characters. And—as he noticed the women in the cast—to see them in their natural beauty before dressed up with stage makeup. Today, he felt two or three actresses looked very interesting.

"All right," Rex Flint said loudly, interrupting Barrymore's musings and the talk of the cast who sat around the stage in their straight-backed chairs, scripts in hand. "We've been over this many times during the past three months and I think you're prepared. So these three days are just to polish your delivery. We'll run through it all from the beginning. Remember, refer to your script only if you can't pull the line from memory."

A rustling of script pages followed his statement, and Barrymore knew they were each finding the page on which they had their first lines. He did the same, and creased the script over on that page. He felt ready. He knew that line of Macbeth's in the third scene of the first act, as he entered and saw the three witches and murmured the words under his breath—*"So foul and fair a day I have not seen."*

But in the first short scene, only the three witches appeared. The director handed scripts to Sarah Bernhardt and Ellen Terry. "Sarah, you're the first witch, as you know, and Ellen is the third witch." He gestured toward the slender, gray-haired woman sitting next to Ellen Terry. "This is Karen Nettles. She's playing the second witch." He waited while the three women quickly said hello and became acquainted.

"Now, cast, we're ready . . . *Macbeth, Act One, Scene One.* You'll have to imagine the thunder and lightning, but now enter the three witches." He nodded at Sarah Bernhardt.

The actress put down her script, a gesture showing she knew her lines, and spoke, not in her legendary bell-like tones, but, given the role of witch, in a gravelly-voice tinged with an undertone of evil. *"When shall we three meet again in thunder, lightning or in rain?"*

Karen Nettles looked slyly at the other two women and said in a crackly voice, *"When the Hurlyburly's done, when the battle's lost and won."*

Ellen Terry, in true good witch form and voice, Barrymore thought, responded, with an ominous tone, *"That will be ere the set of sun."*

They spoke the other few lines of the first scene, and others spoke their lines in the longer scene two and completed it as Barrymore sat waiting patiently to say his opening line in the third scene.

The director and cast had begun the long, arduous process of rehearsals that would consume all their waking hours over the next three days and nights until at last, costumed and deeply into their characters, they walked onto the stage at eight p.m. Thursday night. For him and the others, Barrymore knew, it would seem at once both an instant and an eternity until that magic moment came.

Chapter Eight

Tuesday Afternoon, June 24

Penny arrived at the theater in the midst of the rehearsals somewhat before three p.m. She took a seat next to Darnell and said, softly, "What have I missed?"

"Flint has taken the cast through the first three acts, and act four is about to begin. You missed the three witches in their first scenes, but here they are again."

On stage, Rex quelled the rising voices of actors, saying, "Act four, scene one."

In their roles as the witches, the three gray-hairs began speaking lines from their chairs. Later, a cauldron would be amidst the three, according to the script Darnell held out for Penny to see, but not in this run-through. Certainly in the dress rehearsal the next day. But they spoke as if they stood around the cauldron, dropping ingredients into the bizarre brew.

They'd spoken a few lines, and Sarah Bernhardt as witch one was saying,

> "Round about the cauldron go
> In the poison'd entrails throw,
> Toad, that under cold stone
> Days and nights hast thirty-one
> Sweltered venom sleeping got,
> Boil thou first i' the charmed pot."

Then all three chimed into a chant together,

> "Double, double toil and trouble
> Fire burn and cauldron bubble."

As the actress-witches continued to speak of *"fillet of snake to boil and bake, and eye of newt and toe of frog, and wool of bat and tongue of frog,"* Penny whispered to Darnell, "I love it, but when will Barrymore come on?" She watched the actor as he sat onstage in his chair, turning pages.

Darnell said, "When the hags—you know what I mean—get their pot fully boiling, he enters." He turned two pages over. "Here." The bracketed words [*Enter Macbeth*] appeared.

She listened, and in a few minutes, heard the mellifluous voice of John Barrymore call out from the stage, *"How now, you secret, black, and midnight hags. What is 't you do?"*

The witches answered, *"A deed without a name."*

Barrymore, as Macbeth, went on questioning them, demanding answers, receiving dark replies. An apparition appears and warns, *"Beware Macduff."* In moments, a second apparition said, *"None of woman born shall harm Macbeth,"* and Barrymore answers it, *"Then live, Macduff; what need I fear of thee."*

"His first fatal misjudgment," Darnell said.

He and Penny spoke softly. Soon a third apparition appeared and said, *"Macbeth shall never vanquish'd be until Great Birnam Wood to high Dunsinane Hill shall come against him."*

And Barrymore/Macbeth predictably responded, *"That will never be."*

"His second mistake," Penny said. She sighed, "I'm a bit tired, John. Would you walk back to the Inn with me?"

"Of course. There'll be more *Macbeth* rehearsals tomorrow, including the dress rehearsal. And I'm sure you'll want to see them rehearse *Hamlet* Friday and Saturday."

They rose quietly and walked softly up the aisle to the lobby and across that to the exit and the street. The afternoon sun was slanting at an angle, creating long shadows of buildings on the cobblestone streets. When they reached the Inn and their rooms, Penny kicked off her shoes and lay down on the bed.

"It's been a tiring day or two. A nap is what I need."

Darnell poured a glass of water for her. She sipped it and then lay back again on the pillow. He picked up one of the books he had purchased at Blount's Books and opened it to the cover page. *Shakespeare's Plays: Contemporaneous Accounts, Anecdotal Stories, and Stratford Historical References to the Early Folios.* He opened it to the first page and began to read.

That evening, Darnell arranged for a quiet table for just the two of them in a restaurant a few doors away on Scholars Lane and they talked about things other than ghosts, although the names of Shakespeare and Barrymore did arise from time to time. The pending addition to their family formed the main topic.

"I like the way the nursery's looking," she said, over her fish dish. "I think that sewing room was just waiting to be a nursery. You did a nice job preparing it."

"Sung was very helpful. He has more talent than cooking."

"I'm glad we have everything ready—the crib, linens, nighties. And I love the wallpaper. There's a few things I want to do. Frilly curtains on the window, pictures on the wall."

Darnell nodded. "Pictures a baby would like looking at."

She smiled. "*Baby.* That's a word we'll have to get used to around our home."

Darnell glanced out the window adjacent to their table and said to Penny, "Look. Someone we both know."

John Barrymore, smiling broadly, walked by the restaurant window arm-in-arm with a slender, sensuous-looking woman with long, flowing light brown hair rippling down to her shoulders. She wore a flowery, silk dress with a light black shawl around her bare shoulders. Her eyes were fixed on Barrymore, who faced forward, apparently so his great profile could be admired by her. The couple seemed to be walking toward the Inn.

Darnell said, "That's Felicia Baron, a member of the casts of the plays. You arrived after they were all introduced."

Penny watched them until they were not visible through the window. "Well . . . he's not married, is he?"

"In between, they say. Divorced from his first wife."

"First?" Penny smiled. "Sounds like there'll be more Mrs. Barrymores."

"I think he'd be surprised if there weren't." He mused. "He could do worse than Felicia Baron."

Penny's eyes flashed. "You like her looks? Nice and slender, hmmm?"

Darnell gazed into her eyes, reached across the table and took her hand. "I was thinking of *his* preferences—an actress."

After dinner, they walked through the town, enjoying their leisure time, glancing into shop windows. Upon their return to the Inn, they sat in a corner of its restaurant near the bar area where they'd met the Aylmers Sunday night and that comprised a pub. Darnell took a glass of sherry and Penny a sarsaparilla and they talked over their drinks for awhile. Seeing no one they knew walk by, they went up to their rooms.

John Barrymore closed the hall door of his suite behind him with his heel and in one motion swept Felicia Baron into his arms, kissing her passionately. He was pleased to feel the warmth in her response. "I've wanted to do that since I met you this morning," he said, breathlessly.

"I know," Felicia breathed. "I could feel your eyes on me all day."

"You're the most gorgeous Lady Macbeth I've ever seen," he said, smiling. "You should be on the New York stage. You'd create a sensation." He moved his hands lightly over her shoulders, down her arms in a gentle caress.

She pulled away, laughing lightly. "Where's that valet of yours you mentioned? Is he going to pop in any minute? And do you have anything to drink in this shabby suite of yours?"

"He's in his room, probably asleep. The lock's on my side of the door. And I've made arrangements to have champagne in an ice bucket in my room every night." He moved to the table, removed the bottle from the bucket, removed the cork protector, and twisted the cork until a light pop accompanied the bottle opening. He filled two champagne flutes and handed one to Felicia, kissing her lightly again as she took it from her hand.

"I see they gave you two glasses with your bottle." Her eyes twinkled as she smiled at him. "For whatever unsuspecting actress you inveigle to come to your room."

He took her roughly in his arms, spilling some of his drink in the process, and crushed her lips with his. "I don't think you took that much inveigling, Felicia."

"Let's sit," she said, twisting out of his arms and flopping on one of the two plush sofas in the room. She put her glass to her lips and drained it. "More please."

After Barrymore refilled her glass, drank his own and filled it again, he sat next to her, their knees touching. "All right. You want to talk, I see. Tell me about yourself. Why are you here in this quaint village instead of on a big city stage?"

"Like London? I do have ambitions, John. But you have to

start somewhere. You should remember that, even at your age."

Barrymore grimaced. "I'm not that ancient. Mid-thirties."

She laughed. "Mid, going on forty. But I'm only twenty-six, John." She paused. "I studied dramatics in London. I'm from there, you know. Then this opportunity came up. To do Shakespeare plays all summer. I couldn't resist it."

"You want to be a dramatic actress as a career? I mean, as a life's work?"

"Exactly. You saw Sarah Bernhardt there today. And Ellen Terry. I've looked at their careers. I'd like that life."

"It's the life I lead." He set his glass down and put his arm around her shoulders. "Maybe we could share that life."

She looked at him, with a faint smile playing about her lips. "You mean, you'd move to Stratford?"

He took the empty glass from her hand and said, "Now, you're playing with me. No, on Sunday I leave. Back to New York. But you—after the summer, when your festival's done—you'll be free." He pressed his lips on hers again, excited when she put her arms around his neck for the first time.

She sighed. "Free to be your slave, *Oh, Great Profile?*"

He held her tightly, moving his hands about her body. "I'm serious about you, dear woman." With one hand he reached over and clicked off the lamp. "Let me show you how I feel."

Somewhat after ten p.m., with Penny already dressed for bed and propped up against pillows with a book in hand, Darnell looked up from his book on Shakespeare's plays at the sound of running footsteps in the street below. He peered out, and saw two men running down the lane toward the river. One of them looked like the constable although the dark and distance prevented certain identification, but the girth of the man and a suggestion of uniform seemed to mark him as Edgar Clive.

Something had happened near the river—near the theater, perhaps. The noise abated, but he sat without returning to his reading, preoccupied with his imaginings.

In a few moments, the abrupt ring of the room telephone startled both him and Penny.

"My God, what a noise at this hour!" Penny said.

Darnell quickly dropped his book and picked up the receiver and base of the phone to prevent further ringing. "Professor Darnell," he said into the mouthpiece.

The voice on the other end sounded breathless. "Sorry, Professor—it's Constable Clive. The ghost has been seen again."

"By the river? I think I saw you running there."

"Yes. Near the theater. Two tourists had been walking along the riverbank and the apparition just appeared before them and just as fast disappeared. They called the mayor, and the mayor called me, and we both came down here. Of course, there's no sign of him, now."

"Is the mayor with you?"

"No. He went home. But said to let you know, and that he'd talk with you in the morning."

"Same ghostly appearance?"

"Exactly. The people are staying in town, so they'll be available tomorrow if you want to see them."

"Thanks, Constable."

Penny said, "I heard that. Another sighting."

"Ye-es. I expected it. Whoever it is seems to be enjoying his little masquerade. And he's getting bolder." He paused, thinking. "I'll have some things to do tomorrow, Penny."

She nodded. "I'll watch the rehearsals. I think I've done

enough touring. In fact I've seen most of the attractions of the town."

Darnell smiled. "Except the town ghost."

Wednesday morning, they'd arisen early, had coffee and tea sent up to the room, dressed, and were preparing to go down to breakfast before Darnell went on the rounds he'd planned, when the phone rang. He looked at Penny and said, "I have a feeling that's not just room service." He glanced at his watch—not yet seven-thirty.

Mayor Aylmer's voice on the line did not surprise him. A follow-up call on the ghost sighting, he thought, as the mayor started to speak, but quickly changed his opinion.

"John, I need you at the theater right away. Constable Clive's here with me. Portia Regan's been murdered!"

"Portia Regan. The accident with the curtain weight . . ."

"No accident this time. No question about it. She was strangled. Come back to her dressing room, John, that's where she is. And hurry! This changes everything."

When he hung up, Penny said, "I heard that. The poor woman."

"I have to get to the theater. Let's walk down to the restaurant; I'll get you a table and then go on." For the first time since their arrival, he took his .38 special from his suitcase and dropped it into a side pocket of his jacket. As the mayor said, *This changes everything.* From now on, this was a different assignment. Now it was a murder case.

Chapter Nine

Wednesday Morning, June 25

Darnell entered the Shakespeare Memorial Theater through the stage door, nodding at the constable's deputy at the door, and strode back toward people gathered outside a dressing room.

Mayor Aylmer hurried up, alone, and whispered, "That matter I told you about—I'm afraid the Prince's trip here is off."

Darnell spoke low, "Probably. But you have until Friday. You could wait until we sort this out before calling his aides."

Rex Flint walked up to them. "Our watchman found her this morning. It's horrible! Portia's face . . ."

Aylmer said, "George is examining the body—Doc Geary. He serves as medical examiner, but there's seldom any need."

Darnell peered into the dressing room. A man with a full shock of white hair knelt by the body, which lay on its back, looking at her face and neck. Constable Clive stood near him, gazing down at the doctor and body, watching the inspection. The woman's eyes, staring at the ceiling, seemed filled with fear. The doctor gently pulled her eyelids closed, shook his head, rose to one knee, and stood. His words came clearly out to those in the hallway. "Strangled, all right."

Rex Flint said, softly, to himself, "Just like in *Othello*."

Darnell glanced at him and the others in the hallway—the watchman, stage director Danny Marek, and the mayor. All eyes were on Doctor Geary.

The mayor said, "Go in with me, Professor. Rex, you stay out here and keep anyone else out of the room."

Mayor Aylmer stepped into the dressing room, followed by Darnell, whom he introduced to the doctor. Aylmer said, "George, Professor Darnell has had experience with these things."

Doctor Geary said, "With murder? That's what we've got. The first one I can remember here for years." He wiped his brow.

Darnell said, "What do you think, Constable?"

He scratched his cheek. "Don't know *what* to think. Nor what to *do* either. Doc's right. We don't get many of these."

Darnell said, "Mayor, I'm going to recommend something. A murder of this kind calls for a specialist. Call Scotland Yard. You said you know Chief Inspector Bruce Howard? Get him on the phone and describe this situation, ask him to come right away. I can talk with him, too, if you'd like."

Aylmer said, "Yes, I would. We need help on this."

Flint, listening at the door, said, "You can use the phone in my office."

Darnell turned to Doctor Geary and the constable. "The body should not be moved, and nothing disturbed in this room. If we reach Howard, he could be here by late afternoon and inspect everything. Then you can take charge of the body after that, Doctor."

Geary said, "Yes. That will do. Although it can get rather warm in here."

"Yes. How long do you think she's been dead?"

The doctor gestured at the woman's body. "Face, lips and nails pale. Feet turned blue. That happens pretty fast. Rigor mortis has begun. Body's cool. Stiffening of the eyelids, face, neck, and jaw. It looks like she struggled. That would speed it up. Of course, it's warm in here." He bent down again and reached through a torn place in the loose dress underneath

81

the body and pressed the skin with a finger. He stood up again. "Not much blanching." He frowned. "I'd say she's been dead about five or six hours, give or take."

Darnell nodded with approval. "Thank you, Doctor. The chief inspector will appreciate your good analysis of this."

He looked at Flint. "And the watchman found her . . ."

Flint said, "He usually leaves at five in the morning, but he'd fallen asleep, he said, and it was closer to six. We had him stay on—under the circumstances. You can talk with him." He nodded at Skelton, standing out in the hallway with the stage director.

"And Marek? When does he usually arrive?"

"He's an early bird. Six, never later than seven."

Darnell looked at Constable Clive. "If it's agreeable, Constable, you and I could speak with both of them together."

"Yes, good."

"But first we need to call Scotland Yard."

Darnell, the mayor, and Flint went to Flint's office where the mayor put through the call, and after a short delay reaching Howard, spoke with him, telling the details of the crime, and then handing Darnell the phone.

"Hello, Bruce. Will you be able to come?"

Howard's voice seemed to reflect a mixture of emotions. "I'd send someone else, John, this being my retirement year and all. But I do know the mayor. He showed me some hospitality a few years ago. And, of course, you're there . . . yes, I'll come. In fact I'll leave within the hour. That should put me there about five."

Darnell gave directions to the theater and told him where he and Penny were staying. "I'll get you a room, Bruce. You'd better plan on staying a night or two. Will you have men with you? I'd suggest a couple of sergeants."

"Really? Some kind of special duty?"

"We've had some disturbances here. The locals call it a ghost."

Howard chuckled. "That explains why you're there. But you don't think . . . ?"

Darnell shook his head, although he knew the chief couldn't see him. "No. The killer was very human, no doubt of that."

He hung up the phone after their conversation and said to Rex Flint, "A few questions, now, of the watchman and stage director."

They walked back to the dressing room and found the doctor and constable now out in the hall with Onslow Skelton and Danny Marek. "Just so we get it down right, Constable, shall we go over it once more?"

"Go ahead." Clive looked at Mayor Aylmer, who nodded.

"Onslow," Darnell said to the watchman, "just tell us again, please, when and how you found the body."

Skelton cleared his throat. "I make rounds three or four times a night. Keeps me awake, gives me something to do. The last one is just before I leave, usually five. But I fell asleep and when I woke it was already about six. I hurried through the place for my last round—I always look into all the rooms. I looked in there . . ." he thumbed at the open door, ". . . and found her just as she is. It's a room several actresses use. I went in and looked at her." He shivered. "But I didn't touch her. I could tell she was dead."

"It was about six?"

"Or a little after."

"And then?"

He took a deep breath. "I called Constable Clive, then Mr. Flint, and then Mayor Aylmer. The constable arrived first, and Danny was just coming in. Then Mr. Flint and the mayor."

Darnell turned to Marek. "What time did you get there?"

Danny Marek, a slight but wiry and muscular man with thinning sandy hair, said, "As Onslow said. About half-past six or seven. I don't look at a clock. I wanted to get an early start, with all the rehearsing today."

Rex Flint groaned. *"The play!* What am I going to do— Portia was Lady Macduff. *My God!"* He paced back and forth across the hall.

Darnell said, "Something more important, Rex. Does the woman have relatives here? In Stratford?"

He stopped pacing, shook his head. "She lives alone, here. Relatives in London. A father and mother. A brother."

"I'll call her parents," the mayor said.

"You both knew her. Why would anyone want to kill her?"

Rex Flint shook his head silently.

Mayor Aylmer frowned. "I don't know. But that curtain weight—it was no accident, was it?"

Darnell said, "If his plan was to disguise murder as an accident, maybe he ran out of time. Had to do something now."

When the professor returned to his hotel, leaving the constable's deputy to stay with the body, Rex Flint told the mayor he needed time to think. He asked Danny Marek to carry on, but when the cast was assembled for rehearsals he would make an announcement. Half past eight now, and John Barrymore would be arriving at nine, bright-eyed and bushy-tailed, ready to vault into his lines, not knowing what happened during the night.

Flint cringed at the thought of what the day held, and hurried to his office in the theater building. Things he had to do. Secrets that ravaged his mind. Decisions to make.

The first decision, although difficult, was easier than the second. First, he must replace Portia Regan in Lady

Macduff's role. Erin? Doreen? No—Judith Shandy. She could do, with a wig to cover up her flaming red hair. He'd see her as soon as the cast was ready.

The other gnawed at him. For three months, he and Portia had carried on a torrid love affair, under the guise of late rehearsals, and his wife as far as he knew suspected nothing. But now it might come out—someone might have seen them and feel compelled to talk. What to tell Glenna? Another redhead, with a temper to match. He sighed, realizing he had two choices—tell her nothing of the affair, hoping it would not come out, or level with her now, to show what some might call belated honesty. He decided to take a chance and say nothing. He picked up the phone and asked the operator to connect him to his home.

Glenna Flint's voice came on in moments. He could hear her yawning, as she said, "Rex? What's happening so early? You skipped out without breakfast. God—it's not even nine yet. Rex?"

"I've got something disturbing to tell you, Glenna. It's Portia."

"Oh?"

"She's been murdered. Strangled."

"My God!" He felt the tangible silence in the bedroom at the other end of the phone.

"Glenna . . ."

"I know. I'm taking it in. Did you . . . ?"

Flint bristled. "Did I what?"

". . . you know, have anything to do with it?"

"Glenna . . ."

"Now, don't play innocent. I knew about your tawdry little affair. I thought it would have run its course by now, like all the others, all those other ingénues." He heard the sob in her voice at the end.

"I—I didn't know you knew." Flint steadied himself and sat down at his desk. "But Glenna—I had nothing to do with it, I swear! You've got to believe that!"

"I've got to? You've lied to me, you've cheated on me. Now this—this, *murder*. And I should just look the other way?"

"I didn't do it. Glenna, I was home with you last night." He knew his voice was taking on a desperate note and stopped, took two or three deep breaths. She was saying nothing. "I was there with you."

He could hear the change in her tone. "You're trying to set up an alibi, aren't you? Last night? You know I took sleeping powders at nine and I was dead to the world until you called just now. You could've—oh Rex, I don't know what to believe."

He said, "I'll be home as soon as I can—after the cast arrives and I explain the situation. We'll talk."

He heard a click and the line went dead. "Glenna?" Gone.

Dammit! What else could happen? He reached into his bottom drawer for a bottle and glass. He never drank until after five p.m., British style, country club manners and all that—but he needed some help. He splashed a quantity of scotch into a water glass and bolted half of it down, then refilled the glass. Almost nine. The damned meeting with the cast coming up. He thought of the chant of his three old witches—*"Double, double, toil and trouble . . ."* How right they were.

Chapter Ten

Wednesday Morning, June 25

John Barrymore whistled a Broadway tune as he strode to the theater from the Inn. Felicia had left him at one a.m., and he'd slept like a baby until eight. Three cups of black coffee and a scone put him in even better spirits and he was ready to take on an entire day of rehearsals. As he thought of the cast, he realized something very different would be in place today. Lady Macbeth speaking lines to him on stage would be Felicia Baron, a different Felicia than he met the previous morning. One he had met anew the night before in his room. One who was lovely, teasing, tantalizing. A woman a man could fall in love with very easily, if he weren't careful. Very, very careful.

The Shakespeare Memorial Theater loomed in front of him as he came back to the real world from his dreamy thoughts. All right—rehearsals. Bring them on!

At the stage door, he was surprised to see a uniformed man, not a watchman. A constable? A deputy? The man approached him as he entered.

"Mr. Barrymore? Mr. Flint said I was to take you to him as soon as you arrived. I'm Constable Clive's second deputy—just a reserve man, but there's, well, something unusual today."

"Unusual?"

"I'll let Mr. Flint tell you." The young man led the way to Flint's office, rapped on the door, and opened it for Barrymore. "Go right on in, sir."

The actor could see the director was on edge from the

moment he looked at him. Flint's eyes seemed wild, his hair mussed. The director, normally so composed and in control, shifted a pencil nervously in his hands. When Barrymore walked up to his desk, Flint snapped the yellow pencil in half and tossed it on his desk. "Have a seat, John. I have some . . . bad news."

Barrymore nodded. "I gathered that."

Flint rose and paced back and forth across the room, returning in a minute to his own chair. "There's been a murder, John, right here in the theater. Portia Regan was strangled last night."

"My God! Do they—have they found the killer?"

"No. And we have no idea why it happened. We've called Scotland Yard and an inspector will be here later this afternoon to take charge of the investigation."

"Lady Macduff . . ."

"Yes. Judith Shandy could take her place. But the issue's greater than that. Should the play go on? Should the festival go on? What will the public think, and do?" He looked at Barrymore. "And how do you feel about it?"

Barrymore frowned. "The poor woman. I hope the police find the murderer. But that's not our job, Rex. You direct. I act. There's an old maxim in the theater, and you know it as well as I do. In America there's a corny expression—the show must go on."

He felt Flint's eyes boring into him. "So you'd continue? You'd go ahead with *Macbeth* tomorrow night?"

"You're damned right I would!" Over the initial shock, Barrymore saw things differently now. "I didn't come thousands of miles just to turn around and slink back home. It's a tragedy, yes. But the theater has a great tradition. And personally—if you think this crime concerns me personally, let me reassure you. I'm not worried. No one is going to strangle John Barrymore!"

"The public . . . ?"

Barrymore's lips turned up in a smirk. "It's hard to say this, but the public is fickle and they love sensationalism. They'll come tonight just to be part of this tragic act." He paused. "Shakespeare's plays are full of tragedy—look at *Macbeth* itself. Conspiracy, stabbing, poisoning, death. People don't mind watching that."

Flint sat silently for a moment.

Barrymore went on. "Let's do whatever we can for her relatives. Let's help the police in any way we can. But don't cancel the play."

Flint nodded. "It's not my call, anyway. I have to have this same talk with Richard Latimer. As producer, he and the mayor would have to make the final decision. But I'll tell them what you said."

"What do we do now?"

Flint looked at a clock. "The cast will be assembling on stage. Some of them may have heard. I have to tell them something. John—if you'll go out there, that may settle things down a bit. I have to find the mayor—I think he's still here— so we can call Richard. Then I'll be out in a few minutes to break the news, whatever it is."

Darnell found Penny where he expected to, in their rooms. She said, "I've been watching for you out the front window, John. I saw you come back from the direction of the theater."

He nodded. "I saw her body. A vicious killing. That's why I came back. I want to talk with you."

They sat down, Penny on the sofa, John on an opposite chair, so he could look into her eyes, wanting to be sure of her reaction. "Penny . . . this is a murder case, now. There's a murderer in Stratford-upon-Avon, maybe the last place you'd expect to find one, other than on the stage. I'm worried about you, now."

"Why me, John? I'm far removed from the theater people. John, if you're thinking . . ."

He nodded. "I'm wondering if I should put you on a train back to London. For your safety. For your peace of mind, you know, under the circumstances."

Her eyes flashed. "I'm perfectly safe here. And if you think this kind of news will bother me, just remember all the things I've been through with you over the past seven years. A ship that is sunk by iceberg, a train with spies and a bomb, serial killers, kidnappers—everything."

"You won't go?"

"I'll stay here with you, John." She reached over and put a hand on his. "I know you had to ask. That's the way you are. But our lives aren't separate anymore. They haven't been since we survived the *Titanic*. And now . . ." she rested a hand on her midsection, "we're closer than ever."

He sighed. "All the more reason, but . . ."

"I'll stay right here. Go help them solve this case, John."

"Chief Inspector Howard will be here later today."

"Good. You can work together. I'll talk with the mayor's wife and see if there's anything we can do for Portia Regan's family."

"I should get back to the theater now."

"I know." She rose and put her arms around him. "If I'm not here later, I'll be with Kimberley Aylmer. Just be careful yourself, John. You never know where these things will lead."

As John Darnell walked back to the Memorial Theater, he reflected upon Penny's words, *where these things will lead.* Yes, the simple case of a ghost sighting now involved murder. But what was behind the killing? And what might happen next?

★ ★ ★ ★ ★

The constable's deputy found Mayor Aylmer talking with Constable Clive and the night watchman. Minutes later, the mayor closed Flint's door behind him as he entered the director's office and said, "We have to make some decisions, Rex."

Flint nodded and passed on what John Barrymore had said. In minutes he had the producer on the phone and repeated everything they knew about the murder, citing all the issues as to whether to continue with the play and the festival.

"We can't just shut everything down. We'll continue. Can you handle the casting problem, and deal with your cast?"

Flint assured him he could and, after obtaining Latimer's unequivocal support of continuing, and his promise to come to the theater within the hour, Flint said to the mayor, "I'd better handle the cast by myself."

"I understand, Rex. I'll stay here at the theater for awhile, just to make sure everything's under control."

Flint left his office and headed for the stage. Although he obtained support from the mayor, the producer, and Barrymore, he still dreaded facing his cast to tell them one of their own had been murdered. He found them all assembled, some standing on the stage, some sitting, all engaged in a low buzz of conversation. Barrymore stood talking with some of the actors and actresses.

As he walked up on the stage, the cast settled down and Flint made the announcement about Portia Regan's murder. Waves of shock seemed to ripple among them around the stage amid the exclamations from many of them. Sarah Bernhardt shook her head, speechless, Flint felt, for one of the few times in her life.

"Will the play go on?" someone asked, voicing the question all must have in their minds.

Flint raised a hand to quell the hubbub that rose again

after the question and said the words that came to his mind as he walked over from his office. "Portia's death will be carefully investigated by Scotland Yard, and we have every hope to capture the killer. We know of no reason why there should be any general concern for safety. The mayor and our producer, Mr. Latimer, and our star, John Barrymore, have all said they're prepared to present *Macbeth* tomorrow night as planned. But it all depends on you. Are you willing? Will you continue to rehearse, can we do our dress rehearsal tonight? It's up to you, now."

After a moment of silence, as people looked at each other, a chorus of voices spoke out saying things like, "We can do it . . . I'm game . . . the show should go on."

Flint looked about the stage. "Anyone not prepared to do it? There's no problem if you want to beg off. We'll find a way to get by." No one spoke.

"All right. Then we'll be rehearsing today." He searched out Judith Shandy among the crowd, and said, "Judith would you come up here please?"

When she came to his side, he asked her in a low voice, so no one else could hear, whether she'd be prepared to take Portia Regan's place as Lady Macduff.

Seeming stunned by it all, she frowned and said, "I know all the lines, Rex. But . . ."

"I know how you may feel. We have to dwell on what's needed here. You're my first choice. I know you can do it."

She sighed. "Poor Portia. She'll be in my mind—and in my heart—with every line I speak. But, all right, Rex. I can do it." She paused and took a deep breath. "Just bear with me if I cry in the wrong places in rehearsal today."

Flint announced to all that Judith would replace Portia and added, "We'll take a half-hour or so break, and begin rehearsals at ten a.m. sharp. And thank you all. You're a great cast."

★ ★ ★ ★ ★

Darnell found Constable Clive and Mayor Aylmer at the door to the dressing room with a constable's deputy who stood guard at the door. The hallway seemed to have become much warmer in the time he had been gone to the hotel.

"We'd better take a look inside," he said to the constable.

When they stepped into the room, it was as he suspected. The temperature had risen in the virtually windowless room. "I think her body will have to be moved," he said to the constable. "Doctor Geary made a good examination, and it'll be hours before Chief Inspector Howard arrives."

"The cast will probably be rehearsing on stage," the mayor said.

Darnell nodded. "Constable, could you get your men to take a number of photos of the body and this room, from every angle, and then arrange with Doctor Geary to have it moved to the town's undertaking parlor?"

Clive said, "I'll send one of my deputies to the office for a camera, and I'll call George. We can do it."

"Good. With the heat today, it might be prudent."

The constable walked out to find his other deputy, keeping one at the door. The mayor said, "I'll be at my office, John. If you or Ed need me, just call. When the chief inspector arrives, we'll have a meeting at my office so he can tell us how we can help him."

Waiting for Constable Clive to return, Darnell, alone in the room now, the deputy in the corridor, studied the body again, and scanned the floor for any possible evidence the constable or others who searched the room might have overlooked or might not have retrieved. She wore a loose dress. Her shoes were still on her feet. Her long, black hair naturally disheveled. He picked up each hand, lightly, and examined the fingernails. Some reddish foreign matter seemed to be

under the nails. Had she scratched her killer in the struggle?
It would be very normal if she had. The floor was devoid of
anything that might remotely be called a clue. No convenient
buttons or cufflinks that might point to the killer's identity.
Nothing. Nothing to go on except the possibility of some kind
of witness, someone who saw something around the theater
at, say, about midnight or one the night before. And an examination of the victim's life to search out a possible motive.

Darnell walked back out into the hallway, and closed the
door. "No one in or out," he said to the deputy, who nodded.
And he went in search of the night watchman, thinking he'd
find him at his front desk by the stage door. He'd see what he
could do before Howard arrived. He'd start by talking with
Onslow Skelton again. His desk was not that far from the
dressing rooms and perhaps he heard or saw something that
might help. After all, he thought, that's what a night
watchman is for, isn't it? *Odd that he fell asleep, and that
nothing woke him until six a.m.*

Chapter Eleven

Wednesday Morning, June 25

Rehearsals of *Macbeth* resumed at ten a.m. Rex Flint had more than one thing on his mind—the murder of someone he had shared love, or lust, with for months, the fury of his wife, and his need to carry on with the play no matter what, all the while retaining as much of his composure as possible. He knew he appeared frazzled, but felt the cast would put it down simply to the matter of Portia's murder alone. Judith Shandy took hold quickly of her new part as Lady Macduff as he took the cast back over scenes in which she was involved the day before, in the person of Portia Regan.

He was pleased that Barrymore had taken it all in stride. He and his co-star as Lady Macbeth, Felicia Baron, seemed to be able to generate genuine feelings between them as they again ran through lines they'd said the day before. Repetition, and moving about among the cast members, doing the lines perhaps again, perhaps in a disjointed or out-of-sequence order, was Flint's method for cementing remembrance of lines and movements during these rehearsals. That night at seven, they'd do a complete dress rehearsal straight through the play, with full costumes and props, and that would be the essential test of what he would have accomplished by then in the short time available to him.

Part of him was anxious to bask in the glory of the actual play the next night, considering it a minor miracle of blending the cast together with Barrymore, in his style of acting, in just a few days. Part of him was afraid it could be a dismal failure.

The full rehearsal this night would be the bellweather. As far as he was concerned, whether he went home that night at all to face his wife was questionable. He had a bottle of scotch in his office and a leather sofa. That might be his home after he was satisfied with the dress rehearsal and the cast left at midnight.

His mind flicked in and out of reality as the actors and actresses flew through their lines. Barrymore was now speaking his important act one, scene seven soliloquy he had performed unevenly the day before, showing Macbeth's struggles with questions of right and wrong, his ambivalence and misgivings as to murdering King Duncan. *Murder,* Flint thought, *is with us everywhere . . .*

"If it were done, when 'tis done," Barrymore as Macbeth was declaiming, *"then 'twere well it were done quickly. If the assassination could trammel up the consequence, and catch with his surcease success, that but this blow might be the be-all and end-all . . ."*

But Flint could think of nothing but Portia—her face in life, her long hair, those blue eyes, how her body once felt against his. Then horrible images of her on the dressing room floor came. And he imagined the look on his wife's face when they talked on the phone. He shook his head and concentrated on the stage. Lady Macbeth—Felicia Baron—had entered and was encouraging Macbeth to do the foul deed he contemplated.

Barrymore said, *"If we should fail?"*

And Felicia, as Lady Macbeth, responded, *"We fail? But screw your courage to the sticking-place, and we'll not fail. When Duncan is asleep, whereto the rather shall his day's hard journey soundly invite him, his two chamberlains will I with wine and wassail to convince . . ."*

Women, Flint thought. They were his troubles, too, his

tempters, and maybe his downfall. The depth of his loss, his great errors in dealing with Portia and his wife, continued to crash down upon him.

They spoke on, and he heard Barrymore/Macbeth at last concede, *"I am settled, and bend up each corporal agent to this terrible feat. Away, and mock the time with fairest show: false face must hide what the false heart doth know."*

Rex Flint said, "Good. We'll break for a few minutes." He turned on his heel and headed for his office. That bottle of scotch was still almost full. His nerves could stand a bit of it right now. This day would go well only with a bit of help, to hide his own *"false heart."*

Darnell found watchman Onslow Skelton at his standard post, his desk just inside the stage door entrance where he'd met him the day before. When he came up to him, Skelton yawned and took out his watch in an obvious gesture, saying, "After ten. I should be going home."

"Before you do, just a few questions, Onslow, if you please."

Skelton removed his uniform cap and brushed his thinning hair back with his hands. "A few more minutes won't matter."

Darnell studied him. "You said you fell asleep last night and woke about six?"

"That's right."

"A long sleep."

"Yes."

"Do you often nap at night?"

Skelton looked around the area, but no one else was within earshot of them. "I do. You can imagine—it's easy to do, deathly quiet, no one here but me."

"But last night, someone *was* here. Portia Regan was in

her dressing room and someone went there and killed her. It's not that far from your post here. You heard nothing?"

"No, sir."

Darnell's eyes narrowed. "No sounds of a struggle? Or of Portia crying out?"

He squirmed in his chair. "No. I was asleep." He put his cap back on. "I know I should have been awake. What's a watchman for but to watch. Maybe I won't do this much longer. I don't think they want a night watchman who falls asleep on the job. When Mr. Latimer realizes what happened . . ." He rose with an air of finality and said, "Can I go now?"

Darnell said, "I have no more questions. But just one word of advice, Onslow . . ."

"Yes sir."

"Be careful."

The townspeople of Stratford-upon-Avon would not soon forget the morning of June 25, 1919 in the middle of the Shakespeare sesquicentennial festival. News of Portia Regan's murder traveled swiftly by word of mouth and the town grapevine, and by noon Editor Bill Graham of the small *Stratford Chronicle* frantically published a special four-page edition which went on sale at all street corners and was delivered to hotels and stores throughout the village.

The *Chronicle* told of her short life, her residence in Stratford for several years, the plays she appeared in, and contained brief testimonials by a few friends the editor was able to contact before going to press. But no mention of motive, or suspects, or police procedures, other than to say that Scotland Yard Chief Inspector Howard was due to arrive that day, according to Constable Edgar Clive, who was, for the time being, in charge.

The *Chronicle* went on to say that the body was at the local mortuary under police guard and would not be available for viewing until Scotland Yard released it. Relatives in London, parents and a brother, had been notified by the constable. And then, in an editorial way, the editor added at the end of the article he'd written personally, "Lock your doors at night."

Anne Burghe peered through the window glass of Blount's Books: New and Collectibles. Yes, he was there. She opened the glass door, which triggered a tinkling bell above it, and stepped inside. Two customers stood at a bookshelf in the back. Victor Blount sat behind his counter, a book in his hands. She walked up to him.

"Hello, Victor."

"Anne. No tours today?"

"You heard about Portia?"

"Yes. Terrible . . ." His voice trailed off.

"You and she were close once."

"Is that why you're here—to express condolences?" He stood and laid down the book. "No need. Got over that long ago. She had a new, ah, flame—from what I heard. Plays the field."

"Well, anyway . . . I liked Portia. She was all alone in town, like I am, except when Anna comes. We used to have dinner together once a month, regular." Her eyes filled with tears.

Blount offered a clean white handkerchief to her. "Looks like you're the one needing condolences."

She sniffed and wiped her eyes.

"Now you're here," he said. "I want to ask you about something, get your advice as the town tour expert—maybe the *tourist* expert."

She handed back the handkerchief. "Ye-es?"

"This murder—I think it has commercial possibilities. I'm

thinking of making up a little pamphlet. Maybe eight or ten pages. Describe her, go into some of the murders in the various plays, describe her murder. Maybe they'll catch the killer soon. I could put that in. Sell it here in the shop."

"Why are you asking me?"

"Think of all the tours you handle every year. If everyone bought one of my pamphlets . . ."

"Victor! I can't believe you'd do that. She was my friend, and, and—"

"I know all that. But if they find him, the killer, the pamphlet would have a happy ending—you know what I mean."

"No! Don't count on me selling them for you. What you do in your shop, that's your business."

"I'd give you ten percent."

"No, Victor. You're a—well, a good friend—but I couldn't do that."

He came around the counter and put a hand on her arm. He squeezed her arm gently. "We are friends. Maybe someday we'll be more than friends. And you can count on me for anything you need. Even if you say no. All I'm asking is just think about it." He smiled. "I haven't even written the piece yet."

The afternoon wore on slowly, and it seemed to Darnell that everything awaited Chief Inspector Howard's arrival. He calculated Howard could arrive as early as five p.m., depending on when he left the Yard, and whether he drove or took the train. The body had been moved and was under guard. The dressing room in which her body was found had been locked. Rehearsals were proceeding. Penny was presumably with the mayor's wife. And he now sat across the small round table in the mayor's office opposite Mayor Aylmer and the play and festival producer Latimer.

"Fourteen years," Latimer was saying, "and nothing like this. Then ghosts and now a murder. Right in the middle of our sesquicentennial."

Mayor Aylmer nodded. "A hundred and fifty years since the first festival, and I'll bet nothing like this ever happened before. Certainly nothing like it in my time. No ghosts. Never a murder, for sure."

Darnell asked, "Do you think it could be related to this special milestone year—a hundred-and-fifty years of festivals?"

"If we knew more about her murder, that would tell us." The mayor touched the top of his head of wavy gray hair, in a mannerism, patting it, as if to be sure it was still there.

Darnell said, "When you called her parents . . . ?"

"They said they'd come here as soon as they could. I expect them tonight. Maybe they can tell us something."

"What do either of you know of her—her activities when not in plays, her friends, any problems?"

"One of her close friends," Mayor Aylmer said, "was Anne Burghe. My wife sometimes met with the two of them socially. Lunch or dinner you know. That sort of thing. You've met Anne and could talk with her."

Clive said, "She was well-known in town, at least by sight. Walking to shops, that long hair, very shapely woman. Drew a lot of attention."

"By men."

"By men, yes. But women did not dislike her. Maybe put off by her beauty or occupation as an actress." The constable looked at the mayor as if for confirmation. "The actors and actresses stood apart somewhat."

Aylmer nodded. "They're *in* the community, but not exactly *of* the community."

"Did she have a friend—a man—she was very, ah, close to?"

101

"I know what you mean," the mayor said. "Of course, I didn't know her at all well. My wife did. Speak with her. But Portia seemed very discreet as to her private life."

Darnell sighed. "All of which makes it very hard to construct a motive for the crime. And yet every murder has a motive—and usually a strong one."

The constable said, "If we find what that is . . ."

"Yes." Darnell nodded. "We'll have the murderer."

Chapter Twelve

Wednesday Evening, June 25

At five p.m., Rex Flint released the *Macbeth* cast and stand-ins for dinner with the admonition to be back at seven sharp for the dress rehearsal. Barrymore walked from the theater by the side of Felicia Baron, and said, "Come to my rooms in fifteen minutes and we'll do some private rehearsing."

"What about your valet?"

"I'll get rid of him."

They walked in different directions at the street, and John Barrymore hurried to the Inn with anticipation. Brandon greeted him and asked how the rehearsing went.

"Great, great. Now, Brandon—I need you to go out for dinner. I have a guest coming. And after dinner, just go straight from there to the theater. The dress rehearsal's at seven and I want you there to get your opinion. No one here except you has seen me on the stage and you'll be able to compare this to my work in *The Jest.*"

"Yes, sir. There's a man I met in the lobby today. I'll catch a bite with him. Then to the theater."

"Good." Barrymore watched Brandon quickly prepare himself to leave, and in five minutes the valet walked out the door.

He called down for room service, ordering roast beef and red wine and coffee. He looked about the room which Brandon had kept immaculate, fluffed up the pillows on the sofa, then quickly shaved, changed his shirt, and splashed a bit of fragrance on his face. She'd be there any minute now.

He stepped over to the window and looked down on the street. There she was, swishing along, her long hair bobbing as she walked, toward the entrance of the Inn.

Darnell expected Chief Inspector Howard to arrive any time. He walked back and forth in their room at the Inn, watching for any sign of a car pulling up to the front. Nothing yet. And Penny hadn't returned from her visit with the mayor's wife. Everything seemed to be up in the air.

He heard a noise at the door, a key turning and walked toward it as it opened revealing Penny entering, with a parcel.

"John—have you been waiting long?"

He took her in his arms and they embraced warmly. "How are you? Everything okay? I haven't seen you since break-fast."

She dropped the bag on a chair. "I'm fine. Did you have anything to eat this morning? I know you were rushed."

"I grabbed some lunch later."

"Tell me what's happening, John." She sat in a comfort-able chair, and motioned him toward another.

"Saw the body. Called Chief Inspector Howard—he's coming. Spoke with several people—Flint, a stage director, the night watchman, the mayor, the constable. I'm waiting to hear that Howard has arrived. He's due soon."

"Would you like to have an early dinner? I know the dress rehearsal for *Macbeth* is tonight. I'd like to see some of that. If you're busy, Anne Burghe said she'd go with me. She stopped by Kimberley's late today."

He nodded. "Let's freshen up and go down to the dining room. I can watch for Howard from there."

They had just finished their meal and were drinking tea when Darnell heard the commotion in the lobby just outside the restaurant area. "I think some of our visitors are here," he said, gulping the last of his tea. "I'll be back in a moment, Penny."

Darnell strode out to the lobby, not surprised now to see white-haired Chief Howard's portly form at the registration desk. Two uniformed policemen stood next to him. He recognized Sergeant Catherine O'Reilly immediately, with her short, curly blond hair and trim figure, although he hadn't seen her in almost two years. As he walked up, she and the chief turned toward him.

Darnell extended a hand to the chief and they shook hands. "Bruce. Good to see you. How was the trip?" He turned to O'Reilly and shook her hand also. "Catherine. I see the chief needs you here."

She smiled and said, "He wanted a woman available, just in case. He said, 'What if we have to search the actresses?' I can't imagine doing that, but I wanted to come along."

Howard looked up from forms he was signing at the desk and said, "Terrible trip. We drove all the way. Dusty roads. Bad signs. But we found it."

"You'll feel better after you get into your rooms. Penny and I just had dinner . . ."

"I want to see her," O'Reilly said. She looked toward the restaurant and the others followed her gaze as she watched Penny walk through the doorway and toward them. O'Reilly put a hand to her mouth. "Oh, my!"

Penny walked up, smiling. "I heard that. Yes, we're going to have a baby." She linked her arm in Darnell's. "Eight more weeks."

"Why didn't you let me know?"

"I don't know. We were in Paris for awhile last year, then busy fixing up a nursery. And I guess John's cases didn't bring him into contact with the Yard. But I'm so glad you're here."

Impulsively, she pulled away from Darnell and put her arms around Catherine O'Reilly. "How are you doing?"

O'Reilly said, "It seemed to take forever to get over the loss of my mother. But, well, time moves on. I think of her a lot."

"If you're not busy every minute here, I hope we can talk sometime."

O'Reilly nodded. "I'll see what the chief has in mind."

Howard said, "We'll check into our rooms first. John— what plans have you made?"

"I told the mayor and constable I'd let them know when you arrived and we'd get together at the constable's office."

"Good. Make it seven o'clock. We'll have dinner later."

Anne Burghe came by and picked up Penny just before seven and they strolled over to the theater. Howard, O'Reilly, and the other sergeant, a young man Howard called Art, named Arthur Ramsdell, met Darnell in the lobby and the four walked to Constable Clive's office where Darnell had arranged they'd meet with Mayor Aylmer, the producer of the plays, and the constable.

He made all the introductions when they arrived, and they sat around a table. Constable Clive looked expectantly at the chief inspector.

"The body," Howard said. "I'll need to see it."

"We had to move it because of the heat. It's at the funeral parlor." Clive reached in his desk drawer. "We took photos and had them specially developed for you today."

Howard took the photographs from him and studied them one by one—shots of the body, of the floor, of the room. "Did you or anyone else—" he looked at Darnell, "—see anything unusual?"

Darnell described the examination Dr. Geary performed

on the body and his determination that death could have occurred around midnight or one a.m.

Mayor Aylmer and the constable told Howard about the two ghost sightings and the earlier cat drownings. The constable brought up the subject of the curtain-weight that almost hit Portia Regan and preceded her murder by only three days.

Chief Inspector Howard sat back. He glanced at Sergeant O'Reilly, who had been listening to all of it. "Seems to me," he said, "almost everything happens at night here. The cats. The three ghost sightings. The murder last night. Only the apparent accident happened in daylight, during those rehearsals. And it might have been an accident. No one seems sure. The actress was strangled, no clues were found, no one saw or heard anything—even the night watchman."

"That's about it," the constable said.

The chief inspector glanced at his watch. "Seven-thirty. Rehearsals going on. Actors and actresses streaming out of the theater when they're over, say eleven o'clock." He looked at O'Reilly and the young Sergeant Ramsdell. "What about it, Catherine, Art . . . are you up to a little work tonight, some patrolling?"

When they both nodded, the chief said, "Constable, I think we need to show a police presence in town, along the river, near the theater. Uniformed officers. If you can supply three or four together with Art and Catherine—that should deter any likely ghosts. We'll try it tonight."

Clive said, "I have one regular deputy and three reserve."

"Good. Have them uniformed and here at eight-thirty. You can assign them spots. Meanwhile, I'd like to see the body of the dead woman and talk with your doctor."

Plans set, the mayor and producer excused themselves. The full rehearsal of *Macbeth* was now on their minds.

107

★ ★ ★ ★ ★

By eight p.m., the *Macbeth* dress rehearsal had moved quickly from the play's beginning through the first scene of the third act. Rex Flint felt it was going well. He sat in the first row center, hunched down in his seat, fixing his piercing gaze on first one, then another of the actors and actresses moving about the stage. He was pleased with the costuming and stage direction—Danny Marek had done his usual thorough job. His mind moved quickly with the events of the play's story— Macbeth has murdered King Duncan, Banquo has become suspicious of him, Macbeth is disappointed as he senses that Banquo may benefit more from the murder than he, himself, and is clearly plotting some new crime, while Lady Macbeth wants to put the deed behind them . . .

The producer and mayor who came in late, Penny Darnell, Anne Burghe, the mayor's wife, and local men and women who were steady play-goers allowed to attend by special permission from Rex Flint, watched raptly in the audience. There was Wayne Wyndham, a young, local playwright ambitious to learn all he could before moving to London. Montague Bourne's wife, Carole. Willa Skelton, the watchman's daughter who professed she did not aspire to acting but was always at the theater. Johanna Latimer, the producer's wife, sitting with her husband who had said he might have to leave at any moment to assist the police investigation. Victor Blount, the bookstore owner. And Anthony Welburn, proprietor of the Anne Hathaway Inn who had left in charge his daughter, who was his assistant manager, in order that he might see Barrymore on stage. She'd go to the play the next night.

Other actors and actresses in the Shakespeare Memorial Theater company but not in the *Macbeth* cast also sat in the audience observing, studying, perhaps thinking about their own parts in the second play, *Hamlet*, for which rehearsals would begin the next morning. Flint always insisted on their attendance, and in this case it was enthusiastic.

Felicia Baron, her long brown hair tucked into an austere wig, walked onto the stage from the wing, followed by a minor actor in servant's clothes . . .

"Is Banquo gone from court?" she asks in a voice tinged with fitfulness. She learns that he is, but will return, and then wants to speak with Macbeth, now the King. Waiting, she says to herself, *"Nought had, all's spent, Where our desire is got without content: 'Tis safer to be that which we destroy than by destruction dwell in doubtful joy."*

Macbeth, Barrymore showing his glum mood, says, *"We have scotch'd the snake, not kill'd it,"* referring to the fact that Banquo is now his nemesis. In their talk, he says at one point, *"O! full of scorpions is my mind, dear wife; thou know'st that Banquo and his Fleance lives."*

Flint cringed at the words, thinking of his own wife, Glenna, who would normally be here tonight and whose absence others would no doubt have noticed. One more little thing that would lead to the ultimate disclosure of his activities that he dreaded. He pushed the image of Portia Regan's face out of his mind as he heard Barrymore declaim that before the night was out, *"There shall be done a deed of dreadful note."*

Yes, Macbeth will murder Banquo, Flint thought, but it won't be over. Banquo's ghost will haunt him, just as Portia's haunts me.

The Anne Hathaway Inn experienced an unaccustomed flurry of activity that week, and this night, Serena Welburn, enjoying her responsibility as assistant manager at only twenty-three, wondered what would come next. The professor, a paranormal investigator, and his wife. A chief inspector from Scotland Yard, and uniformed sergeants. And on the outskirts of the Inn's involvement, three sightings of ghosts, and now the murder.

As she drifted around the Inn, noticing tourists in their typical pursuits of dinner, drinking and talking in the pub, gazing at curios and booklets and clothes in the gift shops, she overheard snatches of conversation, which always centered around the bizarre events in Stratford that year.

She smiled, hearing one tourist say to his wife, "I'm glad we came this year, with all these special attractions." His wife sniffed, "Murder is not my idea of an *attraction*, Dennis."

About eight-thirty, the next unfortunate event occurred under the watch of Serena Welburn, who felt particularly young in trying to handle it. A dangerous, wild-eyed man well over six feet tall and wide of body, stormed into the lobby, leading an elderly man and woman behind him straight to the registration desk and to Serena, who was standing behind the desk.

The man's voice, angry and full of emotion, resounded throughout the lobby. "I'm Barry Regan, Portia Regan's brother, and these are her father and mother. Where is she? And where's the constable? And the damn *play* director—what's his name, Flint?" He stood, hands wide on the counter, staring into Serena's eyes. "Can't you speak?"

"Oh, sir—I, I'll get the constable here to see you. I know he'll want to talk with you. And there's a chief inspector here, too, from London."

"Then do it. Get them both here." His eyes narrowed. "And the director?"

Serena knew Flint was directing the dress rehearsal, and could imagine the scene with this large, red-faced man charging up the aisle to the stage. She bit her lip. "Let us make you comfortable in the pub until the police are here. The constable and chief inspector can tell you everything."

Regan looked at the parents, who nodded quietly. Serena took them to the pub and told the waitress to bring them whatever they wanted. "I'll call for the police, now. It won't be long." She paused. "And I'm so sorry about your sister."

Regan scowled. "Someone else is going to be sorry, too."

She left the three at their table, hurried to her desk, and put in a call to the constable's number. The operator said there was no answer. She called a bellhop over to her and whispered urgent instructions.

The boy turned and ran across the lobby and out the door, turning right, toward the constable's office. Maybe they were only out, temporarily. Maybe they'd have returned by the time the boy reached the office. She hoped so.

She looked obliquely at the three sitting at the first table in the pub. The waiter had brought beer for the two men, and tea for the woman. Barry Regan was gesturing and speaking to them vociferously. She could not make out the words, but she heard his tone, and that bothered her. The other thing that bothered her was the bulge in the upper pocket of Regan's coat and the glint of steel that caught her eye when his coat parted for a moment. He carried a gun.

Chapter Thirteen

Wednesday Night, June 25

Following their inspection of Portia Regan's body and a talk with the doctor, the constable, the chief inspector and his sergeants, and Darnell returned to the constable's office just as a bellhop from the Inn ran up to the door. In between taking breaths, the boy told them the news as Serena Welburn had instructed him.

"We'd better get over there," Howard said.

"We'll take my car," the constable said. He and Howard and Darnell jumped into it, leaving the others at the office. In minutes they were walking into the Inn and up to Serena, who motioned to them from the desk.

She walked around it and up to them. "He has a gun—I'm sure of it," she said. "The brother. He's in a rage." She gestured toward the front table in the pub where the three sat.

At that moment Barry Regan saw them in the lobby and sprang to his feet. He seemed to tell his parents, stay here, and charged over to the constable, the only one of the three uniformed. "You're the town constable?" he demanded.

Clive said, "Yes, and I know you're Barry Regan. This is Chief Inspector Howard of Scotland Yard and Professor Darnell."

Regan ignored Darnell and took in the chief and the constable with a wide-eyed glare and his words. "Have you arrested him? The director—that murderer?"

Howard exchanged a glance with Clive. "We're investi-

gating the case, Mr. Regan, and we've just started. I know
how upset you are, but you must not jump to conclusions."
He decided to take the offensive against the belligerent man.
"I'm going to have to take custody of your weapon, Mr.
Regan."

"What . . . ?"

"Your gun. Hand it over, please. And that's not a request,
it's an order."

"You can't . . ." He backed up a step.

"I know you're here to help, but in your emotional condition you could be a threat to innocent people and to yourself.
Now, give me your gun—handle first. And we can avoid de-
taining you in the constable's jail."

Regan seemed to collapse visibly in front of them. His face
sagged and his arms drooped down by his sides. In a moment,
he removed a revolver from his coat pocket and handed it to
the chief inspector. "I—I don't know what I was going to do.
But I had to do something—my sister."

Howard pocketed the revolver and said, "Let's go to your
table so we can talk—all of us. I know your parents want to
know we're doing all we can."

"We want to see her."

"Constable Clive will take you there just as soon as we
speak for a few minutes."

Regan nodded, and he and the others walked to the table
where the man and woman rose as they approached. Howard
breathed better now, hoping he'd quelled the situation for the
time being.

Her parents presented a different picture, the mother
showing tears anew under the strain, the father trying to control his feelings for her sake. But he spoke when Chief
Howard came up to them. "Where's our daughter? My wife—
we want to see her."

"I was telling your son, the constable will take you there. He has a car outside. I just want to assure you both, and your son, that we're doing everything we can to investigate your daughter's—death, and to find the criminal."

Barry Regan recovered partially and said, "You don't have to look far. We know she was seeing that, that director. A married man. I think you can find some damn motives there."

Howard nodded. "We'll talk with him at length tomorrow morning. Things to do tonight. Post our sergeants and deputies about the town." He looked at Portia Regan's mother. "Would you like to go now? Are you up to it?"

She nodded. "I want to look at her one more time."

"I'll see that the Inn prepares you some rooms for when you return."

Clive led the way for the three out to his car and seated them in it. He came back around to Howard who had trailed along behind them. "We had her fixed up a bit by the mortician. Dr. Geary will be there. I called him while you were speaking to her family."

"You'll bring them back, we'll get them into their rooms, and we'll go back to your office." Howard paused. "And the posting of our people?"

"There's still time. Only nine now. We can get them in place by ten, let 'em patrol until midnight. The cast and audience will have reached their homes by then."

"All right. My sergeants and I will grab something to eat while you're there. In an hour, then."

As the car pulled away, Darnell said, "There's one more thing you should know, Bruce. I swore a confidence, but I think I can share it with Scotland Yard."

Each time the subject of death arose in the play's dialogue, it seemed the stage grew darker in tone. Penny observed that even the director seemed to withdraw or cringe at such instances.

In the fifth act now, nearing the dress rehearsal's conclusion, the threads of the story all blended and came together under Shakespeare's master plot. A doctor was remarking about Lady Macbeth, *"What is it she does now? Look how she rubs her hands."* A woman tells him she washes them for a quarter of an hour at a time. Lady Macbeth cries, *"Out damned spot! Out, I say!"*

It was at this point, Penny noticed again how Rex Flint reacted. He had clearly taken the murder of Portia Regan very personally. She wondered at that.

Lady Macbeth went on, *"Here's the smell of the blood still; all the perfumes of Arabia will not sweeten this little hand. Oh! Oh! Oh!"* In the darkened theater, in the illusion created by the costuming and anguished lines projected by the actress, it was hard to remember that this was really Felicia Baron, a beautiful, green-eyed young woman with long brown hair, not the austere and troubled Lady washing imaginary blood from her hands.

The mayor's wife whispered in her ear, "How can they perform like this when they know a woman was murdered right in this same building?"

Penny shook her head. "I don't know, but their performances are intense. They may have an undercurrent of emotion that's driving them along."

Anne Burghe, sitting on the other side of Penny, said, "One year, an actor died of a heart attack and the play went on. Of course, this is different—Portia was one of my best friends. I couldn't do it."

"You knew her well. What do you think about it?"

"I'd like to help find whoever did it. All I know is that Portia had a tendency—well, to become involved with men. Deeply involved."

"You think one of them . . . ?"

"I don't know. I'll let the police and your husband deal with that."

After the Regan family viewed Portia Regan's body and spoke to the doctor, the reality of it all subdued their spirit, and upon their return to the Inn, they took to their rooms, promised by Constable Clive that he'd keep them informed the next day as to the case's progress. They also would face the ordeal of arranging to transport the daughter's body back to London for burial.

"But I want to see Flint," Barry Regan said, as they left Clive and Howard in the lobby, heading to their rooms.

"We'll interview him first. If he consents, we'll ask you in to a meeting—but there can be no accusations."

"I want to know what he knows."

"As we do," Chief Howard said.

Back at the constable's office, he and Howard and Darnell met with Howard's two sergeants and Clive's four deputies. Clive referred to a large Stratford street map posted on his wall and pointed out the six spots where they would be stationed that night and the following night if necessary. "Tonight it'll be ten to midnight, tomorrow from dark to midnight. Watching for any suspicious loiterers, anyone who doesn't seem to belong."

"Any *ghosts*," Sergeant Art Ramsdell said.

Darnell smiled. "Anyone who *looks* like one."

They took two cars, Howard's and Clive's, and all drove to the theater area by the River Avon, and the six took their positions. The constable, Howard, and Darnell walked the entire perimeter of the posted stations, to obtain complete familiarity with the surroundings. Two telephone boxes were

within that perimeter, and the six were told how to get to tele-
phones in the theater building.

"We'll be here for a while. When we leave we'll be at my
office," Constable Clive said. "Call there if anything at all unusual occurs, and use each other for backup if you need it."

The three walked by the front of the theater just as the audience began leaving the building after the rehearsal.

"I'll wait here," Darnell said. "Penny will be coming out."

"Then come to my office when you can," Clive said.

"Say, in an hour."

Howard and Clive drove off just as Penny walked out of
the front entrance flanked by the mayor and his wife and
Anne Burghe. After a brief greeting and positive comments
about the play, the others left and Darnell and Penny began a
leisurely stroll back to the Inn, enjoying the night air. She
went on about the rehearsal, Barrymore's performance and
that of Felicia Baron.

"And you'll watch it again, tomorrow?"

"Of course," she said. "With the large audience, with all
the rough spots smoothed out, it'll be another whole experience. Anne and I will go together again."

"And tonight?"

She sighed. "I'm a bit tired, John. I'm sure I'll sleep well
tonight."

He told her about the Regan family as they walked, and
that he'd spend some time with Howard and Clive before
calling it a night. He saw her to their rooms, made sure she
was comfortable, and strode downstairs and out onto the
street, walking vigorously toward the constable's office. It reminded him of his frequent walks in London, his "prowlings"
as he called them, except for one missing ingredient. The
London pea soup fogs.

As he walked, he again sensed that someone was observing

him, perhaps following him, but after turning and looking back several times, he finally put it down to the natural feelings of suspicion that accompanied a murder situation. He reminded himself this was Stratford, not London, and that concerns should be less here just for that reason alone except for one thing. The small town had produced a murder.

At the office, he and Clive sat across from Howard, who said, "I drew up a list of people I want to see. We'll meet here at nine in the morning and get them down here, one by one."

"Flint, of course," Darnell said.

"Yes—but first, her parents and brother. I want to know everything they know before I confront him. Then Mrs. Flint. And Anne Burghe, a close friend of the dead woman. And the night watchman."

Darnell frowned. "I think he knows more than he's telling."

"And at least one more—this Danny Marek. May know something about that curtain weight accident. And he came to the theater very early that morning, one of the first on the scene."

Clive asked, "And my people—tomorrow?"

Chief Howard said, "I'd say one at your office at all times, three about the town. Tomorrow night, their stations again, because the play will be on. Give them time off in the afternoon." He paused. "Art can join them. I'll ask Sergeant O'Reilly to be present during the interviews to take notes."

At midnight, Howard and Clive returned to the river and theater area to disperse their sergeants to the Inn and their deputies to their homes, giving them their next-day assignments.

Darnell walked back in the deserted streets to the Inn and, in their rooms lit only by a single lamp, found Penny asleep. At that hour, in that light, in her peaceful slumber, she had the look, he felt, of a madonna. Soon, madonna and child.

Chapter Fourteen

Thursday Morning, June 26

As they sat at the restaurant table after breakfast, Darnell and Penny saw Howard, Catherine O'Reilly, and his new young sergeant enter the room. They stopped at the Darnells' table on their way to their own. Howard said. "A busy day, today."

Darnell nodded. "I'll be at Clive's office soon."

"I'm calling the people we want to talk with."

Anne Burghe came by for an arrangement she and Penny had worked out the day before to see more of the countryside and take in the play that evening. "I know you have a lot to do, Professor," she said, when she arrived. "We'll keep company."

"And I'll be leaving now." Darnell said goodbye, wishing them a good day, and strode out of the Inn's lobby toward the constable's office, glancing at his watch. A quarter to nine. The air was cool, and he enjoyed the brisk several-block walk.

Howard was using Clive's phone when he entered, sitting in a straight-backed chair across from Clive in his swivel chair behind his desk. A deputy, Ben Carson, sat at his smaller desk at the window, along with Sergeants O'Reilly and Ramsdell.

Howard hung up. "The Regans. They and their son will be here in a half hour. I called Rex Flint, and he'll be here at eleven. He'll get his night watchman here at one, Danny Marek at two. I'll tell Flint we have to talk with Mrs. Flint—give him that courtesy—and call her in about three or four, or as soon as she can. Then Anne Burghe."

"She's out today with my wife. Sight-seeing."

"Then in the morning for her."

"How do you propose to do the interviews?"

"Informally. You, the constable and I at the table with them. The others over there at the desk taking notes. I won't take notes. That puts people off. They clam up."

Darnell said, "You'll be looking for motivation, alibi, and the time factor in this case."

Howard nodded. "Without physical evidence of any kind, without a witness, as far as we know, we just have the basics."

"Review any suspects from past Stratford crimes . . . look for witnesses . . . check stories for inconsistencies."

"Exactly."

Darnell mused. Still a while before the Regans were due. "I've been tinkering with some theories of my own. General theories about crime, you know. No hard evidence, here, of course, or I'd tell you."

"Go on, John."

"I've found in my previous cases that often a criminal follows a certain pattern, seems to have a rather peculiar or identifiable personality or attitude, or method of conduct." He smiled. "Unfortunately, these ideas have come to me gradually after the fact, and haven't helped with the specific crimes. In fact, they may not help here."

He warmed to his topic and leaned forward, having wanted to broach this to a law enforcement officer for some time. "I call the idea drawing a *profile* of the criminal. Not a sketch, you know—more of a psychological profile, based on my own studies and teaching of psychology and philosophy."

Chief Howard smiled. "You call yourself, what is it—a 'psychichologist'?"

"That's right, Bruce. The 'psychic' part has been related to my work in the paranormal field, but I think there are broader applications of the general idea. The point is this—you study the nature of the crime and imagine features of a criminal that would be consistent with it. Form a character profile of a type of person most likely to commit a crime of that type."

"Like your slashing murders in '17—the 'Ripper' case. A definite type and motivation there."

"Yes. Now here, we have just the one murder. But the idea can still apply, to an extent. Something like this . . ." He paused, collecting his thoughts. "There's no scientific evidence, of course . . ."

Howard interrupted. "I take it you don't subscribe to the theories that criminals have close-set, beady eyes, large ears, or a hawk-like nose. Or that brain abnormality must be the reason for killing. Or that all killers are simply insane."

Darnell laughed. "No, but I imagine those common theories will be around for a while until better studies are made. I think it's the criminal *behavior* pattern that should be studied. And the purpose in a repetitive murder situation would, of course, be to apprehend the killer and prevent him from killing again. We'd look at the type of murder, isolate peculiarities about it, determine whether there's anything like a ritual or habit or trademark in the criminal's method."

"Like using the garrote—in your Paris case?"

"Yes. Later, I concluded the killer wanted to avoid *touching* the victim personally, so used a garrote. In other cases, we might decide a killing was done in rage—for example, when there are vicious, multiple knife-wounds, going well beyond what was needed for the killing, therefore showing great hatred. And some cases with a repetitive killer—someone with deep psychological problems and perhaps motivations even the killer himself doesn't fully understand, might reflect special methods such as tying the victim, or slashing, even torture."

"That's interesting. But you're talking about something far different than we have here—a simple strangling."

"Yes. Those techniques would more likely apply to a string of murders that might seem disconnected but which, with analysis of the crime and speculation about the motivation and behavior of the killer, could point police in the proper direction. And good police procedures could be established to find the killer."

"Reviewing criminal records, looking for a suspect to fit."

"Yes, that sort of thing. But, Bruce, as you said, this is not such a case. Just a strangling. And yet . . ."

"Go on."

"Well, there are a few things that can be deduced, or surmised, even here." Darnell paused. "Portia Regan was strangled. First, whoever did it had to get close enough to her without her screaming—what's the expression, *'bloody murder'*—so he could commit the crime in relative quiet."

"Someone she knew."

"Precisely. Second, the act of strangling is a very personal and emotional way of killing. The murderer could have been emotionally involved with the woman either earlier or now, and was releasing pent-up emotions such as rage or hatred."

"Possibly." Howard scratched his head. "Or there may have been a simple *true* motive. Nothing psychological at all."

"Right. The killer may have wanted Portia out of the way for his or her own special reasons. Money is often a motive. Or it could have been to silence her if she threatened to reveal something, like an affair, to someone else. Or it could have been to remove her from her position as an actress so someone else could step into her shoes. Or perhaps it was to take revenge on her for past actions."

"All right, John. Let's go through all of those. Money? I don't think she had any. To shut her up? Maybe she was going to reveal an affair she was having. Flint? Now, to remove her as an actress—that points to the woman who took her place, Judith Shandy. And revenge—how about Mrs. Flint as a possibility?"

"Yes, those ideas come from thinking about both the *type* of killing and potential *nature* of the killer, as well as including motives. I think it's rather likely that someone who knew her well, someone with a very personal motive, strangled her."

"And what about your ghosts?" Howard smiled. "And the cats that were drowned? How do they fit in?"

"I know—you're saying they don't fit the pattern of behavior or the method of the murder. And you're right. This is where, if you have more than one crime, drawing a murderer's profile—either in your mind, or on a chart—may show strong differentiation in patterns and irreconcilable differences." Darnell looked at the others, noticing they were listening intently to the discussion. "That's why I believe, Bruce, that Portia's murder was performed by *one* person, and the provocative ghostly appearances and bizarre drowning of cats were done by *someone else entirely*. The second person may be dangerous as well, so far only showing a strange behavior pattern, but no violence toward a human. I think we have one *killer,* and another *potential killer*—and they both may be planning other murders."

With his words, the room fell silent until the abrupt opening of the front door and the entrance into the room of the Regan parents and their son, caught everyone off guard.

Constable Clive jumped up, took a deep breath, and walked over to the three people. "Come in, and thank you all for coming. Just, ah, take a seat at the table. We want to hear anything you can tell us, and we have some questions."

Mrs. Regan, breaking out of her obvious quiet character, spoke first. "I just want to take my daughter home."

Her husband rested a hand on her arm. "Yes, we want to do that. I've talked with the mortician about his motorized hearse. He could have a driver follow us to London. We want to leave today with her."

Clive looked at Howard, who nodded. "All right, Mr. Regan. You have our permission."

Mrs. Regan sobbed, then took out a handkerchief to blot her eyes. "Thank you."

Barry Regan spoke up in an angry voice. "Well, I'm not going with them. I'm staying on here until you get whoever— whatever animal killed my sister."

Clive said, "We'd like to ask some questions. The chief inspector is in charge of this case now."

The father nodded. "Barry, be calm now. Let's see what they want. Maybe we can help this way."

Clive nodded at the chief inspector. "Go ahead, Bruce."

Bruce Howard looked at Barry Regan. "You made some serious accusations last night, sir. You called the director a murderer. You said Portia was seeing him, in a romantic way. Do you have any evidence of either one of these statements, any reason for what you said?"

Barry Regan reached in his pocket and pulled out a crumpled envelope. He extracted two sheets of pastel-colored paper and passed them over to Howard. "Read that, especially near the bottom of page two. See what *you* think."

Howard held the sheets up so Clive and Darnell on either side of him could read along with him. The first page described her experiences in play rehearsals, mentioned the imminent arrival of the actor, John Barrymore, told of her desire and apparent opportunity to act in a play with him.

Coming to the final paragraphs on the second page, Howard read them aloud so O'Reilly could note them . . .

Barry, there's something I have to tell you. I've gotten involved with the director here, and now I'm worried. Rex is so hard to resist, and I know my judgment with men isn't that good, but he hasn't been acting himself lately. He's aloof and like a stranger to me again. Not like he has been for months. Mrs. Flint—yes, he's married, but don't dare tell Mom or Dad!—she looked at me yesterday when she came to the theater, and I saw something there that bothered me. Oh, and I almost got hit by a big curtain weight today in rehearsals. I don't want to worry you, but I don't know what to do. I'm in the middle of something that isn't going right at all. Maybe it's my imagination, Barry, but I just had to tell somebody. Like my big brother.

Regan's eyes flashed. "I got that letter in the post Tuesday afternoon. Then yesterday the mayor called and told us she was murdered. Is that evidence enough?"

Howard said, "It seems clear she was worried about their romantic involvement. And neither Flint nor his wife were acting as she might expect them to behave. And of course, the accident. She had a lot on her mind." He looked at Darnell. "But there's no clear evidence of murder, only of her frame of mind."

Regan blurted, "But—"

Howard interrupted. "Be assured, we're going to speak with Mr. Flint today. And Mrs. Flint. But let us do our job. Don't interfere. Help your parents arrange with the mortician for that trip, so they get can away this afternoon. We'll talk later."

The young man looked at his parents, put an arm around his mother's shoulders. "You may be right. I'll do what needs to be done."

Constable Clive asked Deputy Carson to go with them when they drove to the mortuary, and to authorize the release of the body. He scrawled out a note for the mortician and handed it to the deputy.

When they all left, Catherine O'Reilly stepped over to the table, picked up the letter from the table in front of Howard and read it silently. "Poor woman. It was her cry for help."

"Rex Flint has some explaining to do," Clive said.

O'Reilly returned to the desk where she waited with Art Ramsdell to take notes. Gazing out of the window she saw a tall man with the handsome look of an actor, wearing tweeds and a scarf about the neck, striding toward the door of the small building. She turned to Chief Howard and said, "I think the man you're waiting for is here."

Chapter Fifteen

Thursday Morning, June 26

Felicia Baron hooked her arm in John Barrymore's as they walked out of the theater. "Nice to have a break," she said. "Rex doesn't usually give one this early."

"How about some lunch? Do you have a favorite place in town?"

When she directed him, they struck out for the tea shop across town. Barrymore enjoyed the quaint village. Different from New York, of course, and he wouldn't trade the one for the other, but he liked the change. Most buildings just one or two stories. Interesting street lamps. Some streets still paved in the old cobblestones. And a pert young English actress on his arm. Very pleasant, indeed. Lionel and Ethel should see him now. They'd take back their comments about his "wild-goose chase" for fame across the ocean.

One day—and not many years ahead—Barrymore knew he'd be back again. Next time it would be on the London stage. That felt right to him. But Stratford was good practice, and offered plenty of atmosphere to soak into his bones.

"You're quiet, John," Felicia said. "What are you thinking about? The play tonight?"

"No, just reflecting on how comfortable this town is, and how lovely you are."

She smiled. "You should have an Irish brogue to go with all that blarney."

He turned his profile toward her. "Will you come to New York after the festival? I'll introduce you to producers, playwrights, get you on the stage there."

"I do think you're serious. And even if you're not—well, thanks. I'll stay in England. My eye's on the London stage."

He said, "You won't believe this, but I'm thinking about London, too, and a play there. In a few years."

She laughed. "Look me up if you come. Maybe I'll still be available."

Barrymore cringed. The thought did bother him—to go back to America and leave this gorgeous, nubile young woman here. All he could say was, "Now you're teasing."

"Here we are," she said, and pulled him inside the glass-windowed cottage with a sign, Mary's Tea Cottage, over the door. "We'll have a nice lunch and talk about today and to-night. Not tomorrow or next year. That's too far away."

"Tonight, yes. The play. And then after the play . . ."

"Yes, John? After?"

"We celebrate."

Rex Flint settled uneasily into the chair at the table. The presence of so many officials disturbed him. The constable was familiar to him, but the chief inspector and his two sergeants at the desk unnerved him. Darnell was a question mark. But being grilled by police at this time—Portia's death, Glenna's fury—the play tonight. *How much could one man stand!*

He took out a cigarette and lit it. Clive said nothing as Flint deeply inhaled it. He knew the constable didn't like smoke in his office, but he blew it out, toward the ceiling, with a huge breath. Let them complain. *He'd walk out right now!*

The chief inspector cleared his throat. *So he was the one asking the questions.* Flint looked at him.

"A few questions, Mr. Flint. I know you've got a lot on

your mind today, with the play and all. But let me just ask first—what was your relationship with Portia Regan? We have reason to believe . . ."

Flint glared. "What—that we were having an affair? Yes, I admit it. I found out even my wife knew about it. This hasn't been a good week." He puffed furiously on his cigarette, emitting a cloud of smoke.

"Was the affair ending? What terms were you and Portia Regan on, say, the day before she was—murdered?"

Flint knew they had some private information. Maybe Portia told somebody. *Better be careful.* "These things have a life, and then they end. It was mutual. We had stopped seeing each other several days ago."

"After the accident? The weight that almost killed her?"

Trying to shake me up. All right . . . "Before that. Two or three days before."

"Did she accuse you? Of being, ah, responsible?"

"No. Not at all. It was an accident. A pure accident."

"She wrote a letter, Mr. Flint."

He stubbed out his cigarette, for something to do. *Think!* "I had nothing to do with it. Bad ropes. Yes, she may have said something in the moments afterward. She was very frightened. I was shocked, myself."

The chief inspector shifted in his chair. Flint knew the big question was coming. All right.

"Where were you the night Portia Regan was killed?"

"I was home with my wife. In bed. From about eleven or so. Didn't return to the theater until I heard the news the next morning."

"Who told you? What did you do?"

"The night watchman called me. He called Constable Clive, too." Flint nodded at him. "And the mayor. The mayor and I arrived about the same time, between seven and seven-thirty. Danny Marek, Skelton, and the constable were there."

"If you had an argument with her the night before—about breaking up—you can tell us. Did you kill her in a fit of anger? Juries understand those things."

Flint shot up out of his chair. *He knew they were going to ask that one!* And he knew what to do. "No, dammit! We had no argument. I went home as I said. Ask my wife. I didn't kill her. We were breaking up, but . . . well, those things happen."

He sat down again in his chair, shaking. "It was hard on both of us."

"She made it sound like you dumped her, Mr. Flint. In her letter."

He fell silent for a moment. *Must gather his wits.* He took out another cigarette. "I don't have anything else I can add. She may have seen things differently than I did. A woman, you know."

"You offered that we could speak with your wife. We'll do that later today. We'll call her."

"Do that—but I need to get back to the theater now."

Howard glanced at Darnell and Clive, then said, "All right, Mr. Flint. Perhaps we'll speak again."

Flint left the office as he arrived, striding quickly down the sidewalk, this time toward the theater. He wanted to get away from there as soon as he could, put that behind him. He must concentrate on *Macbeth* now. His cast was waiting.

Howard looked at the others and said, "What do you think?"

Constable Clive answered first. "Covering up something. But I never thought of him as someone who could commit a murder."

Darnell said, "He's used to acting, how it works—in fact,

he directs people in how to create false emotions. He was hiding something. But it doesn't mean he's guilty of the murder."

"Doesn't fit your mold?" Howard smiled. "Your profile?"

Darnell shook his head. "Not that. He could fit. But we don't have enough data on that subject. As you pointed out earlier, a number of possible motives come to mind. It all goes back to motive in this case."

"Let's grab a sandwich. The watchman Skelton isn't due until one."

Clive's deputy returned and they walked two blocks over to a café where they ordered sandwiches and coffee. Darnell and the others listened to the morbid information the deputy passed on, how the mortician had made arrangements, calling a mortuary in London, explaining that Portia Regan's body would be transported to it later that day. The mother and father were driving back at two, followed by the hearse.

Darnell said to Clive, "You'd better have someone keep an eye on the son beginning at two."

Clive nodded at his deputy. "Ben'll do it." He turned to him. "Be at the mortuary at two. Barry Regan will be there, I'm sure. Accompany him back to the Inn and suggest he stay there until I contact him later tonight. Tell him to keep away from the theater."

Carson asked, "And my duties after that, Ed?"

"Stay in the lobby of the Inn. Keep your eyes open. Watch the exits."

"We'd better get back," Howard said. Darnell could see the old chief was holding up rather well, but as the day lengthened he could imagine the weariness the other might feel—in his last year before retirement, away from the familiar territory of London and Scotland Yard.

As they walked back to the constable's office, Darnell

lagged back behind the others with Sergeant O'Reilly. "How do you think he's doing?" he asked in a soft voice.

She shook her head. "He looks tired. I know you haven't seen him much these past two years, but since that knife attack by Baldrik, he's not been the same. I'm surprised he agreed to come up here. He puts in a short day at the Yard, these days."

"When is his official retirement date?"

"The last day of December. He wanted it that way. To finish out the year. To be retired when the new year starts."

"A little over six months. This could be his last big case."

"I'm sure of it. Maybe that's why he came. Wanted one more big one." She looked at Darnell. "And because you were here."

Back in the office, Catherine O'Reilly continued to think about the chief as they waited for the watchman to come. She had worked more and more with him in past months as he gravitated toward retirement, doing more detail work, more "leg work," for him on his cases. Inspector Warren seemed slated to replace him, having mellowed after the Ripper case, becoming better with staff, showing her more appreciation.

Of course, she knew Warren would never be like Chief Howard, a man who seemed like a grandfather to her much of the time. Yet she smiled, as she remembered times when he barked orders during some critical juncture of a case. Then she saw some of the old fire of the man that older Yard men told her about. How he was as a younger man, coming up through the ranks, as detective, then inspector, and finally chief. She felt herself gazing at him as he and Darnell conferred at the table.

She turned toward the door when the knock came and the door opened. Night watchman Skelton entered and crossed over to the table to Clive. He removed his cap and said, "Constable?"

"Yes, Onslow, just take a seat. This won't take long. Just to get the record straight."

"Yes, Ed—ah, sir." He looked at Darnell and Howard.

"Relax. Chief Inspector Howard will ask his questions. For the record, you understand."

Skelton nodded and looked at Howard silently.

O'Reilly sat with pencil poised over her notebook.

Howard gazed benignly at the watchman. "You found the body?"

"Yes."

"Just describe what happened—for my benefit. I know you've talked about this before. Routine, you know."

O'Reilly saw that Skelton toyed with the cap in his hands as he spoke, turning it this way and that. She wrote, *Nervous.*

"I admit I shouldn't have fallen asleep. I usually make more rounds, but I must have slept from midnight to six. I woke up suddenly, checked the time, and then went about my last round, before going home. It was doing that when I found her. Opened the dressing room door and saw her on the floor. I knew she was dead. Didn't touch her. Called Ed, the mayor, and Mr. Flint. Waited for them."

O'Reilly noticed he stopped twirling his cap, as if suddenly realizing he was doing it.

"Did you hear anyone, anything earlier that night, say from eleven or twelve to one or two?"

"No. I guess I was dead asleep. They say there must have been a struggle. But with the door closed back there, I wouldn't have heard much. I'm saying, it wouldn't have woken me up."

"Yes." Howard paused, studying him. "Danny Marek ar-

rived just after you found the body. You saw him arrive?
Enter the door?"

"Yes. Constable had just come in, and he was on his heels,
walking in through the stage door entrance. I told him what
had happened."

"You see and hear things there at the theater others might
not. Do you have any idea at all who might have killed her?"

"No, sir, I honestly don't." Skelton looked from one of
them to the next, Howard, Darnell, Clive. "Can I go now? I
didn't get much sleep last night either, and tonight's the play.
I could use another nap."

Clive glanced at Howard, who nodded, and said to
Skelton, "Yes, I'm sure the director will want you awake tonight, Onslow. You can go. Have a good nap."

The watchman grimaced at the word, pulled his cap on,
and walked straight to the door without looking left or right.
Out of the window where she sat, O'Reilly watched him stop
at the street, remove a white handkerchief from a pocket, and
wipe perspiration, real or imagined, from his forehead. Then
struck out in a direction away from the theater, apparently
toward his home.

Danny Marek, the stage manager, arrived within minutes
after Skelton left. "I'm early," he said. "Cast's on a break."

"This won't take long, Mr. Marek," Chief Howard said.
"Just tell us your part in the drama of yesterday morning."

"Drama? Oh . . . well, I came to the theater about my usual
time, six-thirty or so. The constable had just walked in, and I
wondered what it was all about. I found out from Onslow. He
and the constable and I walked back there . . ."

"The dressing rooms were never locked?"

"No. Never. That one was shared by several actresses,
whoever needed it."

"No chance of mistaking one woman for another?"

"What? Oh, murdering the wrong woman? I don't think so. The lights were on in the room. She wasn't in costume—no mistake there. No."

"Do you have any idea who may have done it? There was that accident the previous week—"

"I don't know. The accident—we never knew enough about that. Could have been deliberate, knowing what we know now. Then—it just looked like the ropes were frayed."

"Or cut?"

"Maybe. You might suspect it, now—but I don't know. I'm not an investigator."

"If you hear or see anything else suspicious in the next day or two, you'll let me know? And, by the way, keep your eyes open there will you?"

"Yes sir."

After Marek left the office, Darnell said, "When do you plan to see Mrs. Flint, Bruce? I'd like to be here."

"Of course. I'll call her now, and get her here at five. We'll take a break until then. I want to plan our patrols for tonight. Big night of the play, right? *Macbeth*. Lots of people on the street." He smiled. "Maybe even a ghost."

Chapter Sixteen

Thursday Afternoon, June 26

John Darnell was pleased to find Penny back in their rooms when he returned at three that afternoon. "Finished touring?" he asked after he held her and they kissed. He could feel she didn't want to separate from his arms, leaning her head on his shoulder.

She sighed. "I've seen everything, and it's great. But Anne and I were talking about Portia—so depressing you know."

"Yes. Her parents are taking her back to London today."

"Is there something about these Shakespearian tragedies, John? Some kind of jinx?"

His smile was sardonic. "You know my feelings on jinxes."

"The number thirteen brought us together. Still . . ." She moved away to take a seat on a padded chair with a straight back. "There, that's better on my back."

"Are you feeling all right?" His voice showed immediate concern.

"Oh yes, just found I can sit more comfortably this way." She patted her stomach. "I have an extra bit of baggage here."

He studied her. "It's early for tea, but . . ."

"Never too early for tea. Let's go for a stroll—a short one, though—to a tea shop. We need some time together."

They found a quaint shop a block away that was light and airy, with flowered wallpaper and lace curtains. A comfortable place conducive to relaxing, Darnell thought, still harboring some concern for Penny.

"The curtains remind me of how our nursery will look,"

Penny said. "I'm anxious to finish that room when we get home."

"Maybe you're ready to chuck this trip? Go home early? I could put you on a train, and Sung could meet you there."

"No, John. *Macbeth* tonight. And I really want to see *Hamlet* Saturday. Two or three more days." She touched his hand. "I'll be fine."

"You and Anne have been enjoying each other's company?"

Penny nodded. "She canceled her tours this week to escort me. She mentioned she wanted you to look at her heirlooms, or antiques, whatever they are, when you can."

"I promise I will. But the murder, the investigation, I'm rather wrapped up in it." He paused. "Maybe Saturday morning?"

"I'll tell her that. You know, her family has a long history in Stratford. Her ancestors go back almost two hundred years here. I guess a lot of local families do."

"Any deep dark secrets?" He smiled.

"She hints at things, but is rather private. Still, this is the cradle of Shakespeare, John, and his tragedies like the ones we'll see this week are played out over and over. I think it seeps into the atmosphere. You've had ghosts, strange animal killings, and one murder. I really don't think anything you find here or that happens the rest of the week should surprise you."

After they returned to the Inn at almost five, Penny said, "I could use a short nap. The play's not until eight, and Anne will be here at seven, a little early."

"I'll be back by then, and the three of us can walk over together. I'm meeting Bruce Howard at the constable's office at five. One last interview. Oh—he wants to talk with Anne

137

Burghe tomorrow. Some questions about Portia."

"You take care of it, John. Talk with her when you return." She yawned, kicked off her shoes, and lay back on the bed.

At these moments, John Darnell had the recurring feelings of doubt about bringing her here—in fact, about coming at all. Less than two months until one of the most important days in their lives. *Shouldn't they be at home, safe, in their flat?*

He bent down and kissed her gently, then, seeing she was already dropping off, walked softly to the door and closed it behind him with as little noise as possible. He walked rapidly to the stairs, down through the Inn's lobby, and out onto the street.

Mrs. Glenna Flint looked out the window of the car on her way to the interview—*interrogation,* the police probably called it. She had mixed feelings. Yes, Rex was her husband, and she honored a wifely duty toward him. *But damned if she'd lie for him!* After all the lying and deception she suffered from him during their six years of marriage, all those affairs with his young *ingénues.* When they married, she'd agreed to move with him from London to his new job in Stratford in 1914, willing to give a nostalgic village a chance. She soon found the truth—for her, the town was boring, with no London-style social life, while for Rex it was like a fox hunt, pursuing one woman after another. In a quiet rage, she'd endured the knowledge of that for a year now.

The stage hand driving the car pulled it up to the constable's office and hurried around to open the door for her. She'd told her husband, "Damned if I'm going to walk through town to the constable's office, making a spectacle of myself." He'd provided the driver and car for her.

"Come back in exactly one-half hour," she told the driver. "Not a minute later."

"Yes, mum," he said, and drove off.

She opened the office door and swished inside, fixing her green eyes on the man she knew was the chief inspector, the white-haired, grandfatherly-type from London. She knew Constable Clive, of course, and his deputy. And she'd met Professor John Darnell and his wife, Penny, at the dinner Sunday night. The young uniformed female sergeant from London sat at a desk by the window, evidently an assistant.

"I'm here," she announced. "At your *command*, I might say."

Clive closed the door she had left standing open, and gestured toward the table. "Just take a seat there, if you would Mrs. Flint. Just a few questions. This won't take long."

"You're bloody right it won't. I have to get ready for the play tonight. I haven't even selected my dress yet." *Put them in their place right away,* she thought. She took the seat.

The three men—Howard, Darnell, and Clive—took seats opposite her, almost encircling her at the small, round table. "I feel overwhelmed by all of you," she said. "Are you all going after me at once?"

Clive shook his head. "No, Mrs. Flint. Chief Inspector Howard will ask most of the questions. The professor and I will observe."

She sniffed, fluffed up her bountiful, shoulder-length red hair with a hand, then waited. *Let them ask,* she thought. But the answers I give are up to me.

"We know this is a delicate matter, Mrs. Flint," Chief Inspector Howard began, looking into her eyes. She saw kindness there, and yet a man doesn't become a chief inspector at Scotland Yard without steel in his spine. She'd watch her step.

139

"Murder is delicate? I suppose that's one way of describing it. By the bye, Chief Inspector, how is London? I haven't visited there in two years. How's the fall stage season looking?"

"Don't go to them, myself. Now, Mrs. Flint—" he began.

"Pity. 'The play's the thing,' Shakespeare said."

"Yes. I want to ask you about Tuesday night. Two nights ago. Just simply tell us about your activities that evening, where you were, what you did."

"The night of the murder."

"Yes."

She looked at the other two—the pleasant professor, but not one to be underestimated, and the friendly, nonentity constable. She tried to convince herself she had nothing to fear, yet her hand began to tremble as she talked. "I shopped during the day, and went home. Rex and I had dinner and he went off to rehearsals. I had a splitting headache and went to bed early."

"The time, please?"

"Nine. I remember that distinctly because I took some sleeping powders to help me sleep, and I glanced at the clock. It didn't take long with the powders. Just some minutes."

"So you were asleep by nine-thirty, at least. And you slept how long then?"

She looked at him, knowing Rex had told the man something. "I slept straight through. I do that when I take powders. I didn't wake until the next morning." She saw the men looking sidelong at each other, and wondered what Rex had said.

"What time did your husband come home?"

"I don't know."

"You don't know when he came home?"

"I was asleep. I slept all the way through until the next

morning when he called me from the theater. Well after eight a.m. Woke me up."

"So—once more, Mrs. Flint—you didn't see your husband after you went to sleep until the next day? And you were in bed all that time."

"Yes. You have it right. We each have our own bedroom."

"All right. How well did you know Portia Regan?"

"She was from London. She'd lived here for almost three years, worked in the Memorial Theater all that time, I understand. I didn't really meet her until about a year ago, although I'd seen her on stage."

"She and your husband worked together, as director and actress, on a number of plays?"

"Over three years, quite a few."

"They were friends."

"Oh, come now, Chief Inspector. Don't insult me. They were having an affair. I found that out some time ago. She was the type. Had done it before." She crossed her arms and glared at him, trying to stare him down.

He stared back. "You hated her for it. You went to the theater the week before, tried to kill her by cutting a curtain weight rope. Then Tuesday night you slipped into the theater and found her and strangled her. That's about it, isn't it?"

Her words exploded. "Is that how you do your investigations in London, *Chief* Inspector. Accusing innocent people? Insulting them?" She took a breath. "The answer is no. No, I didn't try to kill her. No, I didn't strangle her." She paused. "As to hating her . . ." she said the words with every good intention of finishing the sentence crisply, but felt tears filling her eyes. She took a lace handkerchief from her purse and blotted them away. ". . . as to that, I was getting numb to his peccadilloes. She was the third floozy I'd found out about. It was beyond hate. I think it was disgust—but more than anything, disgust with him." She looked down as she touched her eyes again with the lace. "And maybe with myself."

Howard waited, obviously giving her a respectful period to collect herself. She appreciated that of the old gentleman. She could collect her thoughts.

"Do you have any idea, Mrs. Flint, who might have wanted to kill Portia Regan?"

"No." She hesitated, then decided to say it. "I know you might suspect me, or Rex. I didn't do it. As to anyone else, I'll leave that up to your investigative team." She glanced over at the female sergeant, who was taking notes.

"Your husband?"

"He may have wanted to, but frankly, Inspector, I don't think he had the spine for it."

When she saw the car pull up in front of the office, she told Howard, "My car's here. Anything else?"

When he said no, she marched to the front door, anxious to get away, and soon sat in the front seat of the car next to the driver. She closed the car door and sighed. "Take me home."

"You were very quiet, John," Bruce Howard said. "No questions."

Darnell nodded. "You asked all the right ones. I was studying her. Quite an interesting woman."

"Could she have done it—I mean, would your profile system allow for it?"

"Of course, yes, from a psychological and motivational standpoint. She had a perfect motive. The scorned wife, the philandering husband, and the young mistress. But I think she's made a decision to leave her husband. I heard that in her question about London, in her refusal to give him an alibi, and, if you noticed it, not giving much comfort to her husband being an innocent party. But she did make sure to clear herself, at least according to her story. Sleeping through the night."

"Yes. Not a wife faithful to the death."

"There is one thing, though, we can't overlook in this. By not giving her husband an alibi, Mrs. Flint also deprived herself of one. She could have gone to the theater herself, while Rex was asleep in his own room, and killed Portia Regan in a fit of rage. Normally you wouldn't think of one woman strangling another, but anger can give you unusual strength."

Howard's deputy brought in the reserve deputies who had just arrived, and he gave them all and Sergeant O'Reilly their stations around the theater area. "Be there at seven. I'll be moving around from one place to another, checking with you. Keep your eyes open tonight. There'll be crowds of people coming from seven to eight, then leaving after eleven." He glanced at his watch. "That'll give us all a chance to have some supper first." He frowned. "Missed tea today. Funny, I just didn't think of it."

O'Reilly came over to Darnell. "How is Penny managing?"

"Enjoying it, the tours, the rehearsals. Napping right now. Of course, we'll be at the play tonight."

"I hope to see her for a while tomorrow."

He nodded. "We'll make a point of it, if you can break away from Bruce."

Howard scowled. "The way this is going, she'll have time. We have plenty of suspects, but no witnesses and no evidence. I'm afraid, John, we could be facing a dead end."

Chapter Seventeen

Thursday Night, June 26

As Darnell walked to the Shakespeare Memorial Theater with Penny and Anne Burghe on either side of him, amid the throngs of tourists and other play-goers, it seemed to him the air held an electric quality. The excitement of a new play could be felt, but beyond that he knew the presence of John Barrymore, about to give his first performance, contributed greatly to the feeling. While not evident, certainly, he felt, the murder of the young actress created some of the suspense and intrigue.

As they approached the building, Darnell saw to the left and right of it at the river's edge, the young Sergeant Ramsdell who came to town with Chief Inspector Howard, and one of Constable Clive's deputies. They were making their presence known. At the door, he was pleased that they were ushered in quickly down to the first row of the orchestra stalls, the best seats in the house, joining others already seated in that row, such as Mayor Aylmer and his wife and Producer Latimer and his wife. Looking about the audience, Darnell also recognized Doctor George Geary; the *Chronicle* editor, Bill Graham; Victor Blount, the bookstore owner; the Anne Hathaway Inn proprietor, Anthony Welburn and his daughter Serena; Willa Skelton, daughter of the night watchman; and Glenna Flint, resplendent in a shimmering green evening gown.

Penny said, "Everybody who is anybody seems to be here."

144

"Indeed." He looked at her. "Are you comfortable? It's a long play."

She smiled. "If I tire, I'll just walk out to the lobby. They'll have intermissions, won't they?"

He nodded. At the moment, the orchestra in the pit played an old Elizabethan air, providing atmosphere, as the seats filled up fast. Almost eight now and the play would begin, but what other intrigues would occur this night? All the players on the edges of Portia Regan's real-life tragedy were here, as well as the players on the stage. The house lights dimmed and the conversations died down quickly as the curtain rose on *Macbeth*. Thunder seemed to come from the wings, and a flash of light, as of lightning, brightened the stage briefly. At its center, he saw the three actress witches.

A made-up and witch-costumed Sarah Bernhardt sat on a chair, her legs covered with a dark shawl. The set was suitably dark and ominous. The other actress-witches stood near her, Ellen Terry, barely recognizable in her makeup and costume, and the local actress, Karen Nettles, slim and gray-haired, also witched-up for the role. Departing from the usual entrance of witches from the wings, they had already taken their places, in deference to the disabled Sarah Bernhardt. The audience broke into spirited applause at their appearance.

Their words skimmed along, gratingly in their witch voices, in the short scene one. Sarah Bernhardt as the first witch was asking now where and why they'd be meeting next.

"Where the place?" she asked.

"Upon the heath," the local actress replied.

"There to meet with Macbeth," said Ellen Terry.

Then, after departing words, they all spoke, setting the tone of the play, *"Fair is foul, and foul is fair: Hover through the fog and filthy air,"* and the curtain descended, no doubt, Darnell thought, to allow time for Sarah Bernhardt to be helped from the stage. The audience responded with an excited buzz of conversation in anticipation of the exciting evening now begun. *And the play was under way.*

Chief Inspector Howard knew this night required him to do work he hadn't done in years—handling outdoor stations of officers staked out to watch for unusual activities and to prevent potential crimes. Not something he'd like to take up again this late in his career as a steady routine. But he could do it this night. In fact, he rather enjoyed the brisker night air after the warm day. And the relative silence and slow pace of the work, despite the underlying tension, gave him a chance to think things through—aspects of the case, and thoughts about his own personal life, each of which intertwined. He hoped this last big case of his would turn out well as he approached retirement, so he could leave the Yard with good memories of his last days.

He stopped first to see Sergeant O'Reilly at her post near the theater, the beginning of his route among his two sergeants and the constable's four deputies. "Anything, Catherine?"

"Not a thing, Chief. I think everyone in town is in the theater right now. I wouldn't mind being there myself."

"Maybe you can catch *Hamlet* Saturday night—if we catch our man before then."

"Do you really think we will? Maybe he'll back off. He can see he's outnumbered."

Howard scowled. "I doubt that he'll show his face while we're here. As soon as we're not around . . . well, anything is possible then. He seems to know his way around town."

"A local?"

He nodded. "That's one thing I'm fairly sure of. Of course, I don't mean someone who grew up here, just a man who's been here for some period."

"You've referred to a man twice."

"I know women are criminals, even killers—but to strangle another woman . . ." He looked over at his next stop, one of Clive's deputies, some distance away. "I'll be getting on. We'll be out here until after the theater lets out and people are off the streets."

He walked along the River Avon's bank toward Deputy Carson. After talking about what to look for and what to expect, he moved on down the river bank, then doubled back at the other stations. It was going to be a long night. And, he had an instinct that nothing at all would be observed out here in the town. No cats. No ghosts. And no killers.

Eleven p.m. arrived, and a few minutes later the audience came out of the theater absorbed in conversations, most serious, the names Barrymore, Bernhardt, and Terry mentioned again and again in the various small groups who wound their through the streets to their hotels and inns, local pubs, or their cars to take them to their village or homes in the outlying areas.

Anne Burghe went her own way along Southern Lane toward her flat on Chestnut Walk, promising to see Penny the next day. John and Penny Darnell strolled up Chapel Lane toward the Anne Hathaway Inn.

"I heard that John Barrymore will stop off in the Inn's pub for a nightcap," Darnell said.

Penny glowed with enthusiasm, and felt invigorated by the play, although admitting she felt a bit weary. "I'd like to congratulate him. He was superb."

"We'll stop by the room, then walk down to the pub in a bit."

They returned to the lobby level and the pub area at half-past eleven, finding some of the local dignitaries there, already with drinks in hand, as well as Chief Inspector Howard.

Howard walked up to them. "Nothing tonight, John. The men and women have gone off to get some sleep. I'm about ready, myself." He smiled at Penny. "I think our police force has scared off the town ghost. Well, I'll say goodnight now."

As Howard walked away, John Barrymore strode into the lobby from the street with a flourish and a woman on each arm—Felicia Baron on one, Ellen Terry on the other. Behind him in a small group followed Producer Latimer, Rex Flint and his wife, obviously putting on a good front of some kind of solidarity under the strained circumstances, other actors and actresses, and townspeople. The happy and boisterous group headed for the pub's bar. Barrymore held a hand up in greeting to Darnell and Penny, and motioned them to join his entourage.

After some jostling at the bar and hurried orders of ale and other drinks, the group of about ten, growing slightly with casual additions of others wandering in, took over a large table in a corner and entered into a babble of conversations.

Penny was pleased to find herself seated on one side of Barrymore. She noticed Felicia Baron on his right, her hand on his arm, and realized for the first time that more than an actor's camaraderie joined those two. She looked sidelong at John, next to her, and he smiled.

When she had a chance, after telling Barrymore how much she enjoyed his acting, she asked him, "How can you go from immersing yourself so deeply into Macbeth's character tonight to adjusting to becoming a totally different Hamlet in just two days?"

He turned his profile toward her. "I've already begun, Mrs. Darnell—Penny. You see, Hamlet holds more for me than even Macbeth. I've thought about it a lot in America, learned all the lines, word for word—a bit unusual for me, some might say—and rehearsed everything about it for months. I've had to put all that in the back of my mind for a few days, but now I can let it out again. We'll rehearse for two solid days. And maybe nights." He glanced at Felicia and smiled.

"You like Hamlet, as a role, I mean?" Penny asked.

"Yes. I feel close to the man, and understand his choices and dilemmas. Deep and dangerous ones in his case, but mirrored in my own life—maybe everyone's life—to a degree. Where to put your loyalties, who to believe in, how to stand up for your integrity and beliefs. Whether it's worth the fight."

"To be, or not to be . . ."

"Exactly, Penny. But on Saturday night, on stage, I will *be*, in a very positive sense." He smiled. "I'll be Hamlet."

Barrymore's valet, Brandon, stepped up and said, "Your rooms are all ready, sir. Congratulations, again. And I'll be retiring to my room, now." He walked toward the stairs.

Barrymore said to Darnell, "Good man. I don't know what I'd do without him."

Darnell nodded. "My valet—actually he's much more than that, runs the whole household, cooks, cleans, all of that—he's been with me for twelve years. I couldn't part with him. Sung's son, Ho San, has lived with us as well for seven years. The boy is seventeen now, and a great help to his father."

Barrymore's expression became serious. "Is this town still dangerous, Professor? After that killing, I just want to be sure no one I'm fond of is at risk." He looked at Felicia Baron.

Penny could see her husband giving that thought before he answered. "There are two answers to that, John," he said to the actor. "First, the crime was very personal, one of rage,

149

one perhaps of revenge or hate. A focused crime. To that extent, that might relieve some of the anxiety all would feel about this. On the other hand, the killer is a murderer, pure and simple, and every murderer is to be feared."

Barrymore's hand found Felicia's and he held it tight. "And so, what should we do? We innocents."

"Go about your work. Be on your guard. And if anything seems suspicious, contact Chief Howard, the constable, or me."

"Nothing happened tonight. Maybe it was an isolated event."

Darnell frowned. "I feel the opposite, that danger may come with the big event of the week. With Saturday's play. *Hamlet.*"

When the telephone rang in their room Friday morning at not yet eight a.m. as Darnell and Penny sat drinking coffee he'd ordered up, a chill went up his spine. *What now?* These phone calls seemed to portend bad news. He answered the phone quickly, before it could ring again, and heard the voice of Chief Inspector Howard.

"John, I'm at the theater. The night watchman has been murdered. Stabbed. Constable Clive called me as soon as he heard. Can you get over here?"

"Of course. I'll be there within half an hour."

He explained it to Penny, quickly dressed, and gulped the rest of a cup of coffee before hurrying out the doorway and down the steps. In minutes he'd entered the theater stage entrance and strode over to the small group—Howard, the constable, and Danny Marek.

"Marek found the body when he came in this morning," the constable said. "He called me over, I called the chief inspector."

"What time did you get here, Danny?" Darnell asked.

"A little later than my usual. About seven." He shivered visibly. "I'm almost afraid to come in by myself anymore."

Darnell turned to the constable and the chief. "The body hasn't been moved at all? Nothing changed?"

Howard looked at the others, who both nodded. "It's just like Marek found it."

"The doctor, George Geary. Have you called him?"

Clive answered, "He's on his way. I called Mr. Flint, too."

Darnell stared at the body, with thoughts flashing through his mind. Onslow Skelton. One-time actor. Here the night Portia Regan was murdered. Said he saw nothing, was asleep.

"What if he wasn't asleep?" he said aloud.

"What?" Howard looked at him.

"The night Portia Regan was murdered. If Skelton was awake, at least part of the time, maybe awakened by the noise, he could have . . ." He paused.

"Seen the killer," Howard finished his thought.

"Yes. And I was just wondering if the killer knew he was awake or not. Probably not. Otherwise he might have dealt with him on the spot."

"Definitely a connection," the chief said. "Skelton knew something."

"Yes, it has to be that way. This killing is connected with the first one."

Chief Howard mulled the point. Darnell could see his thinking process playing out on the man's expressive face. The chief said, "Skelton was blackmailing the killer. He didn't tell us anything in the interrogation, because he had plans. He was planning to meet him here and demand money."

"A dangerous plan," Darnell said. "Not the first time a blackmailer has been silenced this way."

"Damn!" Howard said. "I wish he'd been honest with us."

"Where's the knife?" Darnell asked Clive.

The constable shook his head. "Not here. I looked around for it. Just that deep wound in the chest to go on. Looks like it was a big knife. A sharp one."

Darnell asked Marek, "Did you see anyone here, see anything that would help us in this?"

"No, sir. No one was around the theater at all. I was the first one here. Nothing unusual, except—"

"What?"

"The stage door wasn't locked. I didn't have to use my key. In fact, it was ajar." He shook his head. "Onslow always kept it locked at night."

"He let someone in," Clive said. "Or . . . well, some people had keys themselves."

Darnell said wryly, "That narrows it down to just about everybody in this village. Those who had keys, those who didn't." He turned to Marek. "So, who had keys to that door, as far as you know?"

"Of course, Mr. Latimer and Mr. Flint. Skelton's daughter seems to have had one her father gave her. She came by to see him here sometimes. And some of the key actors get them."

"Oh, God," Clive said. "I'll have to tell the poor girl."

"There's a lot to do," Chief Inspector Howard said, now becoming more official. "The doctor has to give us a report. Constable, I think you and Mr. Flint should see the watchman's daughter together, as soon as Flint arrives. And if you could get a couple of deputies over here to search the grounds outside, there's a chance the knife might have been discarded out there. Also have them ask around in radius of a block or two of the theater for witnesses of anyone entering it last night."

Darnell touched the hand of the watchman. "The body's cool, Bruce. I think the doctor will tell us he was killed at about the same time that Portia was."

Chief Howard nodded. "I know what you're going to say."

"At midnight." Darnell scowled. "While we were all asleep."

Chapter Eighteen

Friday Morning, June 27

The theater came alive quickly as Doctor Geary and Rex Flint arrived and actors and actresses, including John Barrymore, drifted in for their rehearsal call Flint had set for nine o'clock. Learning the news, the cast huddled together, talking about the new murder in small groups on the stage. Producer Richard Latimer and Mayor Aylmer came within minutes of their notification by Constable Clive, who also brought in his men to search the grounds and scout the area for any witnesses.

"We're doing all we can do for the moment," Chief Inspector Howard told Latimer and the mayor, who clearly showed intense agitation, wanting someone to blame. "Doctor Geary has confirmed the method, stabbing—no mystery there. And the approximate time of death as being midnight to one a.m., about as close as he can put it. And the body's been removed."

"But can't you do anything else?" Latimer complained. "Two murders. God! What about our play tomorrow night? What if the audience wants their money back?"

Flint, Darnell, and the constable sat in scattered chairs also in Flint's office, where they held the closed-door strategy discussion. Darnell knew he had to bring up again the subject he'd broached with Howard after his arrival.

"Speaking of ramifications, we need to address an important matter the mayor told me about, and I had to mention to the chief inspector. You know what I'm talking about, Mayor. Do you want to discuss it?"

The mayor groaned. "I've not told you, yet, Rex and Richard. I was hoping, well, that this would be cleared up in time."

Rex Flint and Richard Latimer glared at him in unison. Flint said, "Holding something back? We've got enough mystery."

The mayor said, "It's complicated. The aides of the Prince of Wales called me last Saturday saying the Prince would like to come and see John Barrymore perform Hamlet this Saturday—tomorrow."

"Oh, God!" Flint put a hand to his forehead and shook his head.

Latimer gasped, but seemed speechless.

"When he called I already knew about the sightings of the ghost, of course, and the dead cats," Mayor Aylmer went on. "But it was before Portia's murder. I told him I'd call him Friday, privately hoping the matter of the ghosts would be resolved, and I'd let him know if it was appropriate. I have to call today. But I don't know if Portia's death has made the London papers, or whether the Prince's aide knows about it. And now . . ."

"Now we've got a real problem," Latimer said, finding his voice at last. "Thanks to you, Blake. Dammit, why didn't you tell us?"

Darnell saw finger-pointing beginning. He said, "The important thing is to decide, today, what to tell the Prince's aide who called the mayor." He paused. "I think the mayor should call the aide and report the two murders to him. Lay it out fully. Tell him under the circumstances, even with Scotland Yard here, we can't guarantee his safety—and unless something dramatic happens—he should cancel the trip. Chief?"

Howard nodded. "I agree. We're down to decision time. Can't wait any longer."

Latimer said, "All right. Call him, Blake. But what a loss! To have the Prince of Wales here. It would have been a coup."

"Isn't there anything . . . ?" Flint began, then stopped.

Howard said, "Short of finding the killer—nothing."

"I've got to keep going on the *Hamlet* rehearsals," Flint said. He turned to Latimer. "Are we going ahead with the play, Richard?"

Latimer shook his head. "I don't know what to do."

"The question is," the mayor said, "how do we find the killer? That would answer everything." He stared at Howard, then Darnell and the constable. "You're the experts."

Darnell could see everyone wanted someone else to take the burden of the complicated problems. A new idea had come to him during the talking, going back to the almost-ignored issue of the ghost. He was about to mention it, when Howard said, "John, I think we'd get a better perspective if you'd discuss with us your theories we talked about yesterday."

Darnell nodded. That would tie in to what he intended to say. All eyes were on him again. "I'll give you my conclusions, without all the background. The point the chief and I discussed is that I believe many criminals, certainly killers, have a certain behavioral and motivational makeup that fits the crime. That their reasons for killing come from these factors, not from their physiognomy like beady eyes, a square jaw, or a hawk nose. Or, for that matter, merely from some kind of general madness or malevolence. I call that criminal makeup a profile."

"So how does that help us here?" Latimer asked.

"It leads me to think two different people may be involved. One may be dressing as a ghost for a reason we haven't identified yet. That person very likely also drowned the cats to get attention in a similar bizarre way. But someone else may be the killer—a man, I suspect, because of the nature of Portia Regan's murder, strangling. I think the man's rage shows he knew Portia intimately. Skelton may have identified the murderer and tried to blackmail him. The killing of Skelton was a cover-up—just stab him and be done with it. So, one theory could be that two men are involved, because of their different profiles."

Darnell saw Flint avert his eyes when he mentioned intimacy with Portia Regan. Howard nodded as Darnell talked. And at the end, Mayor Aylmer said, softly, "My God. Two different madmen."

"So what do we do?" Latimer scowled at Darnell. "How do you find two dangerous people—if it is two—when you can't even find one?" He muttered, "I think it could still be one man."

Darnell nodded. "Perhaps it is. But I want to re-explore the ghost issue while police investigate Skelton's murder. I think eventually, one man or two, everything will come together."

"We've seen no ghosts since Tuesday night," Clive said. "Maybe it's past history now, and we won't ever see him again. Maybe our officers around town have scared him off."

"They may have temporarily, but I think he'll be back, because he hasn't accomplished whatever his purpose yet. Rex, it seems to me—and it's my fault—one obvious fact hasn't been pursued. Think of a costumed ghost, out in the village, near the theater. What conclusion might you draw about who it may be?"

Flint nodded. "I see what you mean. It could be an actor."

"I think it most likely *is* an actor, and it's almost *certainly* a man."

"So . . . what would you do?"

"I want to interview every male actor connected with the theater—the chief in charge of it officially, of course. I believe someone with an acting background is the ghost. And Skelton said costumes were stolen from the theater in the past."

"So you find the ghost," Rex said. "In the meantime I've got to do two solid days of rehearsing of *Hamlet*, if it's on." He stared at Latimer. "Well, Richard? Will we do the play?"

Latimer's voice took on an edge. "The play is on—for now. Do your rehearsing. Let the experts find the ghost and the killer—no matter who or what it is or disturbs!"

The ancient parchment sheets lay out on the table before the figure who studied them, then stood, located a magnifying glass, and brought it back to the table to examine the sheets more closely. Eight sheets, obviously pages of a script of a play, handwritten and initialed at the bottom of each page. A lamp on the table, clicked on, better illuminated the pages, which, one at a time, were held up to the light, making the delicate, parchment-like sheets almost translucent.

At the top of the first page of the script appeared a heading, which would intrigue the most blasé reader . . .

Hamlet, Prince of Denmark. Scene—Denmark.
Act 1, Scene I—Elsinore. A platform before
the castle. Francisco at his post. Enter to
him Bernardo—
Bernardo: "Who's there?"

The figure continued to read—for the third time in the past few months—every word that appeared on all of the pages of script, including the write-overs and marginalia notes. The ink was legible, although faint in spots. But the most striking feature of the writings was the initialing at the bottom of each page and a signature at the top of the first page, each of which created anew wild, startling surmises that had nagged the reader's mind since the first examination of the script's dusty sheets when discovered in an old attic chest six months earlier. The initials on seven sheets were *"W.S."* And the signature on the first page read, *"Wm. Shakespeare."*

The woman bundled up the fragile sheets and replaced them carefully in the wooden box in which they had rested for many years. Her mind filled with new determination. Tomorrow that very same play, *Hamlet*, would begin, and it would end that night, and, with that ending, John Barrymore would leave Stratford-upon-Avon the next day. She had to see him before then if she were to accomplish what she wanted to do. Time was running out for her.

But she didn't want to look foolish. She needed someone to examine this script for her before tomorrow night, even with ghosts and murder occupying everyone's attention. As she put the box away, Anne Burghe came to a decision—*if the professor had no time to help her, she knew someone who could.*

With Rex Flint complaining that he needed his office during the organization of rehearsals, Latimer designated his own private producer's office on the mezzanine as a place for the interviews of the actors by Darnell and Chief Howard. Danny Marek agreed to bring actors up one at a time, and co-ordinate their absences with Flint for rehearsals for those who were cast in *Hamlet*. When not in a particular scene, they would be taken to the office. Others not in the cast would be brought up also.

As Bruce Howard and Darnell waited, the chief said, smiling, "What is it about you, John, that seems to attract ghosts?"

John Darnell laughed lightly. "It's the other way around, Bruce. And yet sometimes, like on this trip, I wonder . . ."

A knock on the door announced the arrival of the first actor. The door swung open, Danny Marek inclined his head, and the first man entered the room—a regal, gray-haired man, with a white fringe around the edges of his ears. Montague Bourne.

"I'm Polonius in the play," Bourne said to Darnell, nodding to the chief. "And I've run through my few lines in the first two scenes. My first big speech, of course, is in scene three, act one. *'And these few precepts in thy memory look thou character . . .'* You know, his advice to his son, Laertes."

"Yes," Darnell said. "Good advice, that, too to give a son." The word, "son," took him to thoughts of Penny and their child-to-be. Would he, someday, be giving similar advice to his own son, going off to a university, or into national service, or to America? He shook his head—*must get back to reality.*

Darnell said, "I'm sure you know we're interviewing all the male actors here, not singling anyone out."

The chief added, "You're not under suspicion."

Bourne nodded. "I understand. Fire away with your questions."

Darnell began, "Do you know anything at all about the person masquerading as a ghost?" He watched the man's reaction to the direct question.

The response was mild and conversational. "Nothing, I'm afraid. I've heard about the sightings, that's all."

"Then have you overheard any conversations here, inside the theater, about the ghost?"

"Just discussion. Banter. Jokes. Nothing that would point to anyone. But . . ."

"Yes?"

"Well—from the description of what he wore, I'd say you're on the right track. It must have been someone from the theater who, ah, borrowed a costume or two for the occasions."

"Yes. And the cats?"

Bourne shuddered. "Horrible thing. I have two Persians of my own. To think of someone doing that . . . it's just too cruel."

They released Bourne shortly, and waited for the second actor, who was brought up very quickly by Marek. From the elder Bourne, they now faced a young actor, Reid Perkins.

"I'm Rosencrantz," he said, and laughed. "Well, not really. Reid Perkins."

"Have a seat, Reid," Chief Howard said. "We're just asking questions, not accusing anyone of anything."

"I know. Nothing bothers me. Death on stage or backstage. It's all life, isn't it?"

Howard exchanged a glance with Darnell and went on, "Just tell us first—have you been masquerading as a ghost? Having some fun? Just need to know, lad."

The young man's eyes narrowed, as if in thought, but answered readily enough, "No, not at all. Haven't done it. Not guilty, your honor." He smiled.

Darnell asked, "Anyone you suspect of doing it?"

His head shook. "No. Sounds like fun, though."

"And do you like cats?"

The man's eyebrows went up. "You think our ghost killed the cats? Doesn't sound like what one of our people would do, and I know most of them pretty well."

"If you hear anything, let one of us know."

After he left the room, Howard frowned. "Do you think we'll learn anything from all this?"

"You're the policeman, Bruce. If it weren't for your snooping and interrogations and eye witnesses, you'd have a hard time catching any criminals. You know that. The art of physical evidence hasn't come into its own yet. Even finger-prints . . ."

"I know. No central file. If it's someone close, someone in the family, and you have a good print at the crime scene, yes, you can compare it to all those of the family, maybe find one of them that fits. Otherwise, it's an exercise in frustration."

After a quick knock on the door, Marek brought in Avery Ainsley, tall, obviously muscular under his loose clothing, with long, wavy brown hair. Darnell recalled that Flint had described him as a lead actor, one who would have had Barrymore's roles in *Macbeth* and *Hamlet*, the theater's usual star, had the New York actor not come over. Some jealousy, there?

"Everyone is telling me what parts they play in *Hamlet*," Darnell said.

"Yes, I'm sure we're all proud to be in a production with John Barrymore, whatever the part. I play the king—not a very sympathetic part, I'm afraid."

Darnell nodded. "You'd normally play Hamlet, I suppose."

He smiled. "You mean if Barrymore weren't here? Yes, I would. I've played the part. *'To be, or not to be' Hamlet*—that's the question."

"Won't you miss the spotlight?"

"It's only one time. Then he leaves, and things return to normal."

"Speaking of that, what do you know of the person acting as a ghost here?"

"I wouldn't do it. Could ruin a career. Of course, someone wanting attention, notoriety . . . but, I don't know who it is."

"You've been here for some years. You knew Portia Regan. Do you have any insights as to her murder, or Skelton's?"

Ainsley smoothed back his hair. "Portia was a lovely girl, a bit too loose with her, ah, charms, if you know what I mean. I don't know who'd kill her, or the watchman. Someone who has lost control of his faculties. I just hope it isn't one of us."

Barry McClintoch came into the office next. "I'm not in *Hamlet*," he said, "I played in *Macbeth*. So they asked me to come up now while they're rehearsing."

Darnell thought the man's Scottish accent fit Macbeth very well. "How long have you been here with the acting company?"

"I came down from Scotland three years ago. Love it."

"You acted there, too?"

"Yes, but to be here in Shakespeare's town—that's a real pleasure."

He revealed little to them in their interview. Darnell began to feel that although the questioning was necessary, not much would be learned. Yet they continued on with James O'Bairne, another import, an Irishman with an accent to match, a new player in the troop only a year. He offered nothing new.

Then Philip Dennis, a middle-aged man who seemed to have soured on acting, sat with them for a few minutes and ultimately revealed, "I'm leaving at the end of the festival. It's other work for me, now."

Erik Berg, a man about the age of Reid Perkins, Darnell guessed, entered the room next. "I'm the other half of Rosencrantz and Guildenstern," he said. "Reid and I are a set, you might say."

Darnell caught a trace of accent in the young man's voice. The international flavor of the cast struck him as interesting. "Do you like acting here?" he probed, looking for some new approach that might reveal something useful.

"Beginning my third year. I joined the company in 1917.

Couldn't get into the war, with my disability. Eardrum."

"It doesn't bother you on the stage?"

"We speak quite loudly up there."

"You were in *Macbeth*? Your face looks familiar."

"Yes. Not a big role." He looked down. "From play to play, some roles are small, some larger. I hope to move up."

The chief took over and asked what had become the stock questions about the ghost and cats, and Portia Regan and Skelton, but they learned nothing. Additional interviews followed with actors Andrew Trask and Pierre Gaston, with no results.

Stanford Vance, the last actor on the list of the current company Flint had given them, finished their schedule for the day. "I want better parts," he said. "That's my complaint. I've talked to Flint, but they seem to want a bit of gray hair to put you in the top spots. At twenty-five, I may have to wait for years. I've talked with Mr. Barrymore—he's very helpful. Said I should go to America."

"Will you go?"

"I don't know. I—well, I'm in love with Willa Skelton, and now her father's dead—I have to think it through."

"You knew her father. Why do you think he was murdered?"

He shook his head. "I don't know. He wanted the best for Willa. Wanted her to go into acting, but that was a sore point with them. She just wanted to marry and have a family. She wanted to marry me."

"What did Skelton think of that?"

"He was a former actor. Wanted it to run in the family. But Willa said, let my sons be actors. I think he was resigned to it. Also, he didn't have much money to sponsor her training."

After Vance left, Chief Howard looked at Darnell across

the table they had used for their interviews. "Well? What do you think?"

"I think we've got one day left, Bruce. For some reason, I sense that things are building toward the play tomorrow night. It's the high spot of the week. Better have your people out in force tonight and tomorrow."

"For the ghost . . . or the killer?"

"If they're two men—for both of them."

Chapter Nineteen

Friday Afternoon, June 27

After receiving a call from John late in the morning, Penny Darnell knew it would be a long, difficult day for him. She was anxious to see him, but resigned herself to waiting until he returned to the Inn for dinner. She wondered if the dress rehearsal would go on that night. He told her he'd be out on the streets of Stratford that night, joining in whatever actions might produce evidence of the killer's identity.

As it neared noon, another call came as she sat reading in their rooms. Anne Burghe asked about Darnell, and when told the news of the watchman's murder and Darnell's deep involvement in the case, asked Penny if she could see her for lunch.

"We could eat right there at the Inn," Anne said. "I have something I'd like to talk with you about, so it'll be my treat."

"Please do come. I'm bored to death in this room."

Agreeing to meet her in the dining room at twelve sharp, Penny bustled about, freshening in the bathroom, changing into a flowered dress. She left a note for John, in case he came by, and walked down to the restaurant. She found Anne Burghe already waiting at the entrance, and the host took them to a table.

"It's horrible about the poor watchman," Penny said, when they were seated. "Did you know him?"

"Every local did. He was an actor once, you know. I've seen him on stage, some years ago. He had an accident. Became the watchman. Now—well, it's really sad. He has a daughter, a beautiful girl, even looks like an actress, but she doesn't want to be one. She confided in me, and . . . I think she's in love."

"Who is it?"

"A young actor. Stanford Vance. Her father didn't approve of him—or rather, of the marriage. He saw it as keeping her from the stage. I think he wanted her to do what he couldn't."

"What'll she do now?"

"I don't know. Her mother has been dead for some time, but I believe she has other relatives somewhere."

The waiter came, and after they glanced at the menu, they ordered their food and tea. As the room filled with diners, Penny heard bits of conversation about the murder.

Anne looked about the room. Although the tables nearest them were not occupied, she lowered her voice as she spoke to Penny. "This thing I wanted to talk with you about—you remember I said I wanted Professor Darnell's advice on something?"

"Yes. Antiques, I believe you said it was. I told him about it. But his mind has been on all these other things."

She nodded. "I know how busy he is. By the way, they aren't antiques. They're, well, antiquities, in a sense. Papers. Old papers. Maybe valuable ones."

"I'll remind him. Maybe he could do it sometime tomorrow?"

"I'm afraid he'll still be involved with the investigation. The week has gone by so fast, and with the two murders and everything . . ."

"You sound anxious, now."

"I just wanted to see Mr. Barrymore tomorrow, before he leaves, after I had a chance to talk with your husband."

"So—it involves the stage, in some way?"

"Yes." She frowned. "Oh, I don't want to be too secretive, Penny, it's just that I'm worried about what to do."

The waiter brought their tea, rolls, and salads. After a moment, Penny asked, "So, what will you do?"

"There's another person I could see."

"Do you trust that—person?"

"I don't know. There was a time—but that was awhile ago. I just have to do something."

"Is there anything I can do to help?"

The waiter brought glasses of water and put them on their table. After he walked away, Anne said, "I want to see Mr. Barrymore before he leaves town, and I heard he may pack up after the play tomorrow night and leave Sunday. So I'll see that, well, other person and try to reach Mr. Barrymore tomorrow before the play."

Penny smiled. "I think you want to sell something to John Barrymore."

Anne sat back and stared at Penny. "You're a detective just like your husband, aren't you?"

"Not really. But you were going to tell me whether I could help with your mystery."

Anne Burghe took an envelope from her purse and handed it to Penny. "It's sealed, and has information that might be important if anything happens."

"Happens? You mean, happens to you?" Penny's eyes widened. "Anne, that's beginning to sound dangerous. Don't do anything foolish."

Anne waved a hand in the air. "No, no. I'm just overly-cautious, I'm sure. With the responsibility of my daughter, no husband, and alone a lot—I think I exaggerate things."

"Well, with everything that's happened in this town, you're entitled to be careful. But, as soon as I see John, I'm going to talk with him about all this." As Penny put Anne's envelope in her purse, and despite the mid-day warmth of the room, a shiver crept up her spine.

John Barrymore and Felicia Baron returned from a lunch break taken when Flint dismissed the cast for an hour with orders to return promptly at one p.m. By the time they walked through the stage entrance, they had talked about every angle of the murder.

Felicia said, "It's almost a relief to get back to the discipline of the acting, the lines, and being up on the stage."

Barrymore frowned. "Going from real murders to imaginary ones from the mind of Shakespeare? Not a cheerful change."

"I know you didn't expect anything like this when you decided to come to Stratford-upon-Avon."

Standing in the lobby with her, no one in sight, he pulled her into his arms and kissed her warmly. "I didn't expect to find you, either, Felicia. And I'm glad I came."

She pulled back after a moment and looked about the room, then into his eyes. "You have quite a line, Mr. John Barrymore—a definite line."

"It's the truth, Felicia. The plays are important, but you're more important. To me, the most important thing in life is love."

She rested a hand softly on his arm. "Be careful with that word, John. We're not on stage, you know."

The sound of hurried footsteps coming toward them down the hall disrupted their talk. Barrymore turned to see Flint approaching, accompanied by a tall man with tangled red hair, his collar loosened, and a leather suitcase in one hand, looking as if he might have come from some minor adventure of his own. Pens and pencils stuck out of the man's coat pocket. Barrymore and Felicia looked at each other and waited for an explanation, which was not long in coming.

"John," Rex Flint said, "this is Sandy MacDougall, reporter from the *London Times*. He just arrived after driving up from London this morning. He's been looking for you."

Felicia winked at Barrymore, as if to say, *good luck*—and walked slowly toward the wings. Barrymore muttered, "That's all I need now—reporters."

MacDougall extended a hand saying, "I'm an admirer, Mr. Barrymore, and I promise I won't disturb you. I was planning to come up for *Hamlet* tomorrow night, but when I heard about the murder of the actress—well, I came earlier. And now there's this second one."

Barrymore nodded. "Yes, but don't expect much from me. We have police handling it—Chief Inspector Howard and John Darnell."

MacDougall said, "I know them both, and I'm looking for them. My editor's going to want to get my story on this right away."

Barrymore glanced at Flint. Trying to get away from a reporter was not his usual mode. He knew how important publicity was, but this time he was anxious to be free of prying eyes and questions. He and Felicia didn't need any negative publicity. Carrying on a romance with murders going on . . . ? He wanted a chance to get away and asked Flint, "Rehearsals about to start?"

Flint answered, "Yes, John. Go on up to the stage, if you will. I'll stay with Mr. MacDougall until we find the chief and John Darnell."

As Flint was speaking, Barrymore looked past him to the stage door, seeing Chief Howard walk in with Darnell. "Here they are," Barrymore said. "Good hunting, Mr. MacDougall."

John Darnell stopped in mid-stride as he saw MacDougall standing next to Rex Flint. Chief Howard, next to Darnell, groaned softly and said, "The press has found us."

"I heard that, Chief," MacDougall said, smiling. "What do you expect with a murder—now *two* murders—plus ghosts, and the world's only paranormal investigator prowling around Stratford-upon-Avon. This is news."

Darnell stepped forward and shook hands with MacDougall. "Just arrived?"

"Yes. Seemed to take forever—those roads." He shook his head. "I expect you and the chief will fill me in on all this?"

Howard grumbled, "We're trying to find a killer, Sandy." He sighed. "But we'll tell you what we know that's suitable for public consumption. May we use your office, Rex?"

Flint nodded. "Use it. I have to get over to the stage."

The three walked toward Flint's office. "I hope you're not going to interfere with our work," Howard said.

"I'll actually spend most of my time on the streets, talking to the people of Stratford, or interviewing some of the key people involved. Mr. Flint said he'd talk with me later today. And there are others I need to see."

They settled into seats in the office and MacDougall asked, "Chief, if you could take me through the dates, times, names, and backgrounds of the murder victims first, that would help a lot."

Howard did that for some minutes with Darnell adding a word here and there, MacDougall scribbling furiously in his notebook. When the chief seemed to come to a stop, MacDougall turned to Darnell. "And the ghosts? And those cats?" Darnell spoke of that, and ten minutes later, as MacDougall's questions dwindled, Darnell felt the reporter had about all he needed for his story.

MacDougall folded up his notebook, sat back, and looked at the two men opposite him. "Now, what are you holding back?"

The chief stood, as a signal the interview was over. "Whatever it is, Sandy, it's instinctive on my part, not intentional. You know the basic facts. Now we have to concentrate on the crime. Go do your other interviews."

MacDougall stared at them and shrugged. "I'll find out the rest the hard way, I guess."

Darnell asked, "Are you staying over?"

"One night. I have a room at a small hotel down the street. It'll be my headquarters. I'll do my interviews with Flint, Barrymore, the constable, the mayor, some locals and tourists, write stories in my room, and call them in. I'll see you later."

Chief Howard and Darnell met in Constable Clive's office with the constable, two regular deputies, two reserve deputies, and the chief's two sergeants, Catherine O'Reilly and Art Ramsdell. The constable filled cups for them with either tea or coffee brewed in the small back office adjacent to the single, unoccupied jail cell.

"Here we are again," Constable Clive said, "and no further along. In fact, we have *another* body now. Chief, I'm worried."

"We all are. But, specifically . . . ?"

"Are these killings going to go on and on? We just don't have crimes like this in Stratford." Clive, glum-looking, stared out of the window.

"Tonight could be a turning point, Bruce," Darnell said. "We need a plan."

"We're going to station everyone we have here throughout the town. Including you and Constable Clive and me, that'll be nine." He pointed at the map of Stratford on the wall. "We'll be spotted strategically and spread out so we cover the whole downtown area. And I want two of us inside the theater this time."

The constable pressed, "But what do we expect to do?"

Darnell said, "We've seen that this man—or these *men,* if there are two—are very bold. Going about town in a ghost costume more than once, showing himself—*wanting* to be seen. Drowning those cats, and the animals could have done some wailing while he hauled them about. And the two killings—both there in the theater, the first even when the watchman was right on the premises. The killer could have found himself trapped there, but he took the risk. Yes, bold is the word. And maybe tonight we'll see more of him taking risks."

Howard scowled. "He was seen, or heard, by the watchman sometime on the night he strangled Portia Regan. A witness. If only Skelton had told us what he knew."

Darnell said, "He paid with his life going after the money. And then our killer took another big chance killing him right there in the theater."

Howard nodded. "So—if he's out on the streets tonight, showing himself in costume, or involved in another killing— is putting our people out there the right idea?"

"It may help. We've got to stop him somehow."

Clive said, "A third murder—that's what I'm afraid of."

Chief Inspector Howard nodded. "We all are. If he comes out again, we have to get him first."

Chapter Twenty

Friday Evening, June 27

John Darnell took Penny across the lane and down a block to a quiet restaurant for dinner. "I wanted to get away from the crowd at the Inn. Police, theater people, even inquiring tourists. This is better."

"I like it, John. It's nice to be with you. I miss you."

He frowned. "I know. I wish this was just a vacation trip. It seems like we never have just that simple thing."

She kept her voice low answering, "Yes, always a ghost or a dead body, no matter where we go."

"We'll be back in our cozy old flat soon. I feel things are coming to a head, now. Tonight. Or tomorrow by the time *Hamlet* is over. It all seems to be centered around this week."

"The week that John Barrymore's here . . ."

He stared at her. "I haven't thought of it exactly that way, tied to Barrymore. But it may have affected the timing. I'm sure Barrymore will be leaving as soon as he does *Hamlet*."

Penny reached in her purse and pulled out the envelope Anne Burghe had given her. "I want to tell you about this, John."

The waiter came, and they ordered appetizers and tea. Penny watched him walk away. "Anne gave me this at lunch." She told Darnell what Anne Burghe had said about valuable papers, something connected with the stage, that might involve John Barrymore. "Another Barrymore connection."

"I'm sorry I haven't seen her yet."

"That's what worries me, John. She gave me this envelope—obviously with a letter inside—and said she'd see someone about her valuable papers, someone I really think she doesn't trust completely."

He drank from his cup and sat quiet for a moment while Penny nibbled on the appetizers. He asked, "Is Anne coming to the *Hamlet* dress rehearsal tonight?"

"She said she might be a bit late. It starts at seven."

"Invited guests, again? A small audience?"

"Yes."

"An officer in the theater will know where I'll be. When she arrives, tell her I'll break away to see her if she wants."

"She'll appreciate that. And, John—so will I. I don't want to see anything happen to her."

"So—let's order some real food, now."

The theater buzzed with more than usual excitement that night. Penny knew the invited special guests and dignitaries enjoyed, as she did, the privilege of seeing the play in a form not quite final, not totally polished, in a more intimate setting than before a large audience Saturday. She was pleased to be seated next to Sarah Bernhardt and Ellen Terry on the one side, with a vacant seat on her left saved for Anne Burghe.

She looked around the orchestra section of the theater where the special group assembled in front rows. Almost seven p.m., and no sign of Anne yet. Penny wondered if Anne was seeing that mysterious person, presenting her valuable papers for evaluation. She hoped there was no real danger, as Anne hinted there might be, and that it was simply caution brought on by all the events of the week in the otherwise quiet town.

Ellen Terry turned toward Sarah Bernhardt, smiling at Penny on the other side of her, obviously including her in her remarks, saying, "You should be up there as the queen tonight, Sarah. It'd be a better play if you were in it."

Bernhardt laughed lightly. "I could say the same about you, Ellen. A mutual compliment society. We played our old hags in *Macbeth*—and I'd say, type-cast. Let the younger actresses strut and fret." She put a hand on Terry's. "I'll tell you—that was my last turn on the stage. Now it's over, for me." She turned to Penny. "We're leaving for London in the morning. I'm glad."

"I'm sorry you'll miss *Hamlet*."

Straightening her one leg and shifting on the seat for comfort, Bernhardt leaned toward her. "We'll see this, tonight. I like dress rehearsals. And I'm tired, my dear . . . by the way, I read about your acting turn, two years ago, Penny. The *Ripper* matter, Bernard Shaw, all of that."

Penny smiled. "I hope I got good reviews. At the time, I just hoped to get out of it alive."

Sarah Bernhardt nodded. "People still talk of it."

Ellen Terry said, "Whenever I see my old friend, Bernard, he tells me all about it once more. He's as proud of his role in that case as he is of any of the plays he's written."

Rex Flint walked out on the stage, causing a short burst of applause. He raised both hands in the air. "Ladies and gentlemen." He waited a moment, and repeated the words. The noise subsided and the hall soon fell relatively silent.

"Ladies and gentlemen . . . it has been our custom to invite some of the Stratford community to see dress rehearsals on occasion, and this is a very special one, with Mr. John Barrymore from America playing Hamlet." Another spurt of applause followed this, and he raised his hands and went on. "This is not the final show—that's tomorrow night, and I hope you'll be here for that, also—so some of the costumes and stage settings may not be totally complete, and you may hear an actor fumble a line." Some of the audience laughed lightly at that. "Mainly, we ask that you observe and enjoy, and applaud when you feel inclined, but realize this is not the final performance, and may have a few rough edges." He paused, stood straighter, and said, "And now, we're proud to present the dress rehearsal for *Hamlet,* starring John Barrymore."

As Flint walked off the stage, the house lights dimmed, and the curtain slowly raised, amid applause from the audience. On stage, before them, they saw a representation of dark castle battlements. The audience heard distant footfalls, and a soldier, Francisco, on guard watch, stood more alert as someone approached. *"Who's there?"* Francisco said. He and another soldier, Bernardo, coming as his relief, challenged each other, and remarked about the cold at the hour of midnight.

Penny turned toward the aisle, seeing someone coming, then edging into the seat next to her. Anne Burghe. She smiled at Penny and whispered, "Sorry I'm late."

Penny whispered back, "It just started. Did it go well?"

Her voice low, Anne answered, "Yes. Everything's fine. He—my friend—glanced at my papers. He'll inspect them carefully tomorrow." She nodded at the stage. "Let's watch."

Horatio and Marcellus had entered, conversing, when a ghostly figure slowly came on stage. Marcellus said, *". . . it comes again!"* and Bernardo answered, *"In the same figure like the king that's dead."*

Penny whispered, "Ghosts in town, ghosts on stage."

Anne Burghe smiled, and said softly, "Well, it is William Shakespeare country."

Outside, by the bank of the River Avon, surrounded in a small circle by his sergeants and the constable's deputies, Chief Inspector Bruce Howard also said the word, "Ghosts.

Yes, we're looking for any sign of anything like that. But, remember, it's a killer we're really looking for, so be careful. Two murders, and I want to keep it at that. And I certainly don't want any of you to fall victim. You have guns—use them, if you need to."

Constable Clive asked, "And if we just see someone looking suspicious?"

"We'll all have to use judgment. Try to distinguish danger from suspicion. If you want help, yell out, and the closest one of us will hear you, then we'll come. Draw your weapon if need be." He smiled. "But it's a dark night. Don't shoot one of our own."

Darnell glanced at the sky. No moon—in the new moon phase. And a cloud cover as well. It reminded him of that same kind of dark, moonless night on the *Titanic* when it struck the iceberg. He glanced at his watch. "Shall we move out to our stations, Bruce?"

Howard nodded. Darnell gave what he hoped was a smile of assurance at Sergeant O'Reilly, whose post was to be where they were standing, some dozen yards from the theater, and who remained where she stood. He was content with Penny's safety knowing Howard's Sergeant Ramsdell and Constable Clive were walking back to the theater, one to be in the lobby behind the orchestra section, and the other just inside the stage door where the watchman, not yet replaced, had formerly maintained his post. The others walked along Southern Lane toward Bridge Street to the left of the theater and toward Chestnut Walk to the right.

Darnell proceeded to the right along the bank of the River Avon to a point beyond Chestnut Walk where they had agreed the farthest perimeter of their patrol could be established. He reached the spot, a dark area, shrouded by trees on either side of the river. Although it was a summer night, the overcast conditions and a slight breeze off the river made for a cooler evening in July than might be expected.

He decided to move about a bit, to walk ahead, then back, and to glance at the other bank of the river as well from time to time. If someone expected to create any mischief, he knew it could come from any source, perhaps the least likely. The time passed slowly, and he thought of Penny, inside the theater, enjoying the rehearsal. Was it a bad decision to bring her here?

With time on his hands, his thoughts drifted back and forth between the matter at hand and his concern for her. He clicked open his watch for the third or fourth time. Half past eight now. It would be a long, and possibly a lonely, night out here.

Abruptly, he heard the sound of loud voices down the lane, closer to the theater. Someone had seen something. He heard the sound of shoes clopping back down from Southern Lane and across from Chestnut Walk. In line with what he and Howard had agreed earlier, he would stay at his post, the farthest away.

He knew that if anyone was in serious trouble, he'd hear more about it. He stood still, listening. The footfalls receded in the distance and the shouting stopped. It seemed whatever the sighting or disturbance it had been satisfied or quelled, as most of the others converged on it. He reflected that he'd heard no woman's voice, so evidently Sergeant O'Reilly was not involved.

Abrupt silence followed, in which he could clearly hear the crickets along the riverbank, and the slight splash as of a fish that might have surfaced on the water. Then he heard the second sound, which came softly and swiftly from behind him. As he turned, he realized it, too, had been the sound of a man running, but in this case across the grass next to the river. As he began to turn, trying to reach for his coat pocket and his revolver, he heard a voice commanding him, "Don't touch it. One more move and you're dead."

He turned slowly, but not raising his hands higher than his waist, holding them steady at his sides. Before him stood a man, a young man, wearing Shakespearian garb, his face touched up with white makeup. The voice sounded familiar. The face . . .

"You're wondering who?" The other smirked, holding a pistol leveled at Darnell's chest. "Don't let the makeup fool you. That's for effect. It's served its purpose."

"What do you want?"

The man said. "I have what I want. You. Professor John Darnell. Ghost hunter, correct? Here is your ghost. The Stratford ghost."

"I remember your voice."

"You should remember. We met today. You know me as Erik Berg."

Recognition dawned in Darnell. The young actor, the one who paired with the other young man, Perkins—Guildenstern to Perkins' Rosencrantz. "Yes. Berg."

"But not really Berg, after all." The actor's eyes took on an evil glint. "Think back in your cases. A man you killed, cowardly, shooting him down like an animal. A man you had already put within the shadow of the gallows. Think, brilliant Professor."

Darnell stared at him, the square jaw, remembering the Teutonic accent. A German. Then it came to him. *Baldrik!*

"I see you know. Yes, Baldrik. I'm Ubel's brother. Erik Baldrik."

"But you're an actor, not a murderer. Your brother—he was a vicious killer. The 'mutilator' they called him. And for good reason. Do you know of his terrible crimes? How he hacked and killed with his knife, attempted to murder more than one innocent person, conspired in the kidnapping of the Prime Minister's daughter? You don't know your own brother—a vile man."

The other's lips tightened. "Go on. Do your last ravings. It won't help you."

Darnell could see more of Ubel Baldrik in the young man as he stared at him. Not with the bulk of Baldrik, shorter, trimmer with an actor's style, but with the same cold eyes and evil smile. *Must keep him talking,* he thought, *throw him off . . .*

"All right. I know you're upset with your brother's death. But why carry on his crimes yourself? What do you hope to gain?"

The man's eyes narrowed. "It's called revenge. And I've been planning it a long time." He paused, regarding Darnell as a cat might regard a mouse, ready to pounce on it. "Why do you think there were sightings of ghosts in Stratford-upon-Avon? A place where I just happen to be working as an actor? Did it not occur to you a time would come in your career when you'd be lured by a ghost to your doom? This is that time. I knew if I created a scare in Stratford at the time of the Shakespeare festival, one man would be drawn here. You. As I said, it's you I wanted. I got you here, acting as a ghost. And now you'll pay for what you did to Ubel."

Before the young Baldrik finished his last sentence, Darnell saw the man's grip tighten on his pistol and knew he had only seconds to act. He lunged forward, grasping Baldrik's right wrist and pointing the gun away from them with the force of his attack, throwing his body against the other. The two fell, Baldrik backward, Darnell on top of him. Baldrik attempted to turn the pistol back toward Darnell, whose grip held as he managed to bring his other balled fist up to crack the man under the chin.

Although stunned, Baldrik apparently drew from some reserve of strength born of desperation and forced Darnell over and under him. Although Darnell still gripped his wrist, Baldrik slowly and relentlessly brought his gun around until it almost pointed at Darnell's chest. With his other hand, Baldrik grasped Darnell's throat, throttling him. Then the hand and open fingers released his throat and reached up toward Darnell's face and for his vulnerable, unprotected eyes. But from his own inner resources, Darnell himself turned the man's gun-hand wrist and the gun itself with as much strength as he could muster. Suddenly a loud explosion tore into the air and echoed across the river water. Baldrik's body went limp, the gun loosened in his no-longer firm grip and the man not moving.

As Darnell lay still, breathing hard, gasping, he heard the sound of running feet on the nearby lane, more than one person running. He moved out from under the dead weight of the actor's body and pulled himself up to a sitting position. He looked at Baldrik's face, the dead eyes staring. From his hand, Darnell took the pistol and tossed it aside on the grass. Two men ran up—one of Constable Clive's deputies, and, following him, puffing heavily, Chief Inspector Howard.

Howard came up to Darnell. "Are you hit, John? We heard the shot."

Darnell shook his head. "He shot himself in our struggle. He's dead."

Howard bent down and checked for the non-existent pulse. He turned back to Darnell who was standing now, and stood himself to face him. "We know who he is—Erik Berg. We caught the other one just a few minutes ago."

Darnell's eyebrows went up. "The other one? Who?"

"Reid Perkins. Dressed as a ghost. When we captured him—he's alive, just banged up a bit—he was quick to blame it on Berg. Said the idea was Berg's."

"What idea?" Darnell frowned. "Tell me all of it."

"Perkins said Berg talked him into it. 'Put on ghost costumes,' Berg said to him. The idea was to go out along the lane, by the river, and pretend they were the disappearing ghost in different areas. Perkins thought it was just a stunt. They'd finished their last turns on the stage."

Darnell shook his head. "Chief—take another look at Berg. I know we both saw him earlier today. Doesn't he look familiar?"

The Chief examined the body again, peering into the dead face. "Ye-es, but who . . . ?"

Darnell said, "That man is Erik Baldrik. Ubel Baldrik's younger brother."

Howard looked at the body again. "My God! Yes, I can see it now—the resemblance. This is too much. I don't understand."

He looked at Darnell for an answer.

"Remember how I was forced to kill Baldrik finally, in the *Ripper* case? His brother was already here then, working as an actor. He immediately marked me as a victim two years ago and laid his plans carefully. It was simple enough—lure me up here by acting as a ghost. He knew my reputation. And when I got here, he'd simply kill me, after carefully explaining why, to make his revenge sweeter."

"Revenge? A killer like Ubel Baldrik?"

"Killer or not, Erik was his brother."

Howard looked down at the body and turned then to the deputy. "Go get a car, Ben, and another man. We'll get the body to Doctor Geary. Nothing to examine here."

As Ben Carson set off at a run back toward the theater, Howard said, "In getting you up here, the young Baldrik got an assist from the mayor."

183

"I think he planned it that way. Create enough disturbance during the sesquicentennial festival, with John Barrymore coming from America—I think he knew someone would do something."

"The ghost idea was bait."

"And I walked into the trap."

Howard sighed. "It's over, John. We've got our killer."

Darnell shook his head. "But why would Baldrik kill Portia Regan?"

Howard frowned. "I know your feeling. Can the case really be over? But, remember—you said the killer would have to be someone who had a personal relationship with her. A young actor with a killer's bloodline, a beautiful actress, both in the same theater? It's all there. When you're back at the pub with a sherry or two under your belt, you'll see it's true. Another Baldrik, another killer. Just like his brother." He wiped his brow with a handkerchief. "It runs in the family."

John Darnell glanced at the body again, then stared out gloomily at the shimmering water of the River Avon flowing by. Inexplicably, he shivered in the night air. "You may be right, Chief. But I want to talk with Perkins. And with Flint and maybe others about Erik Baldrik—or Berg, as they know him—and Portia Regan. See if they think it could have happened the way you put it."

The car pulled up and they loaded the body into it. Ben Carson and the other deputy drove off, and Darnell and the chief walked back toward the theater. Howard said, "Clive took Perkins to his office. You can see him there."

Darnell gazed ahead as they approached the theater, seeing people leaving by the front doors and walking out to the street. "The rehearsal's over—and there's Penny with Anne Burghe." His step quickened.

Chapter Twenty-One

Friday Night, June 27

Penny raised a hand in greeting to Darnell as he came near her and Anne Burghe. As he reached them, her eyes took in his disheveled appearance and red marks on his neck. She looked from him to Chief Howard and back.

"John! What happened?"

He took her in his arms. "It's over now. One of the actors here was living under an assumed name. It was Ubel Baldrik's brother. He's dead, shot with his own gun."

"He tried to kill you—oh, John!"

"It's safe, now. His body has been taken away."

She clung to him as he said to the chief, "I'll see you soon at the constable's office."

As Howard nodded and walked to a waiting car, Darnell said to Anne Burghe, "Would you walk with Penny to the Inn?"

"You're not coming, John?" Penny looked into his eyes. "Is there something else . . . ?"

"I just want to talk with the director for a few minutes. Then after I go see the chief again, I'll be there. It won't be long."

"I'll stay with her until you return," Anne Burghe said.

Darnell watched them walk down the lane toward the Anne Hathaway Inn, then turned toward the theater. He could see Rex Flint standing just outside the entrance with some of the townspeople. When he walked up to them, Flint said, "Let's go to my office. I know you want to talk."

Darnell said to the mayor and Danny Marek, who stood with the director, "If you could come along for a bit, that would help."

A few minutes later, they had settled in seats in Flint's office with the door closed. Darnell said, "You've all heard about Perkins and Berg?" When they indicated they had, he told them about Erik Baldrik's deception, how he had been using the name of Berg as he acted in Stratford, and how he'd made plans to lure Darnell to the town at this critical time of the festival, with John Barrymore here. "He wanted the maximum impact of what he intended to do. All along, I was his intended victim."

"Thank God he didn't get you," Mayor Aylmer said.

Darnell shook his head. "But what I need to know is any information at all about Eric Berg—Baldrik, as we now know him—and his relationship with Portia Regan. What can you tell me?"

Flint said, "You're wondering why he killed her?"

"*Whether* he killed her—and, if so, why."

"Surely it was him," the mayor said. "That much is clear. And the motive? We may never know why. Some tawdry affair."

Darnell said, "Danny? You're around the actors and actresses all the time. What can you say?"

He pulled on his ear with thumb and finger. "Well—yes, I've seen him with her, one time. I stopped by her dressing room, and he was in there, leaning against the wall, just looking at her. When he saw me, he left quickly. Of course, I've seen other bees buzzing around her, too." He glanced at Flint and the mayor, then lowered his eyes. "Lots of honey there."

Darnell scowled. "Rex?"

Flint spread his hands apart. "I—I don't know. I've seen

the two together once or twice, but then I've seen others in the company together, too. They chum about, you know, form couples and cliques, these actors and actresses."

"Ever see him violent? Acting strange? Devious?"

Flint shook his head. "No. He was maybe a touch apart. That could have been the accent. We were all sensitive about that kind of thing during the war, you know, and even now."

"But could he have killed her? As director, Rex, you've been close to all these people. What's your flat opinion?"

Flint said, "Who ever knows someone totally? He was under a false name. In the heat of the moment, could he do it in anger, as a result of jealousy? Yes, I suppose it's possible."

"It was him," Mayor Aylmer said, in a firm voice. He stood up and stretched. "The case is closed—thanks to you, Professor. I knew you could do it."

Darnell sat back, glum. He pulled out his empty pipe and stuck it between his teeth, making no motion to fill it. He chewed on it for a minute while the others looked at him. At last he rose also and said, "I have to talk with Perkins at Clive's office." To Aylmer he said, "We could meet for breakfast at the Inn in the morning."

The mayor said, "Good. Nine a.m. I'll be there."

At this hour, Darnell appreciated the chance to walk in the night air the half-dozen long blocks to Constable Clive's office, hoping the walk would clear his mind of cobwebs.

In the now-familiar office of the constable, the local officials and Chief Howard and his people greeted Darnell with nods and compliments. Sergeant O'Reilly said, "I'll bet you're glad the other Baldrik brother is gone."

He nodded, as he took a seat at the table. "They were a bad pair." He looked at Constable Clive, who sat with his feet propped up on his desk. "Perkins is in the jail cell?"

Clive said, "Yes. I suppose you want to talk with him. We already have."

"If you could bring him out for a few minutes . . ."

Clive gestured to one of his deputies, who rose and walked toward the cell. In a few minutes, Perkins was seated at the table opposite Darnell, handcuffed, and with a somber look on his face.

"Tell me about your part in this, Reid. I know you've talked with the police—I just need to know."

"I'm innocent," Perkins said. "I didn't know anything about Berg—Baldrik, they call him now. We'd chummed around a bit over the time we've both been here in the company—the odd glass of ale in a pub, you know. But I didn't know his real name."

"Did you ever see him with Portia Regan? Were they having any kind of intimacy?"

"If you mean, were they sharing a bed, I don't know that either. He was friendly enough, talked with the men and the women. Naturally, more with the younger actresses. But—no, nothing special. Nothing I saw." He smirked. "But that's the kind of thing you keep under wraps, isn't it?"

"How did you happen to get involved in this stunt tonight?"

"It was his idea—Erik's. He said, we'd have a bit of fun, no harm done, just dress as ghosts and show ourselves around town for a few minutes, right after our last lines in scene four of act four—a few scenes before the play's end."

"You went one direction, Baldrik the other."

"Right. We left the theater and split up. He went farther down, said he wanted to find a good spot. After the play, we were going to meet in a pub."

"You know he tried to kill me."

"But I didn't know he planned to. I think he just wanted

me there for a diversion." The young man's face was drawn and lined with worry. "My acting career's probably over, and I'm stuck in this jail. Just because of a little fun." He looked at Clive.

Darnell stood and said, "Well, thank you, Reid. And Constable—I'm finished."

When the man had been returned to his cell, Chief Howard said, "Seems innocent enough. All you have on him, Clive, is disturbing the peace."

Clive said, "I've talked with Rex Flint, and he needs Reid for the play tomorrow night. He'll need to substitute someone else in the dead man's role. I'll let Reid cool his heels here tonight and send him home for breakfast in the morning. He's a good lad, really—just anxious to make a name for himself."

"He's done that," Darnell said.

Chief Howard asked, "Are you going back to your hotel, now?"

"Yes. Penny's waiting. We can walk back together. A few things we should talk about."

Darnell, Chief Howard, and Sergeants O'Reilly and Ramsdell strolled slowly toward the heart of town after leaving Clive's office. Chief Howard said, "You've got something on your mind, John. Out with it."

"No one has a greater understanding of the Baldrik mentality than I do, Bruce. Erik was a junior version of his brutal brother. But he was not into crime, as such. Not a mutilator like Ubel Baldrik. He was an actor, and showed signs of trying to live a normal life. Except—well, even though his brother was an escaped, convicted criminal in the shadow of the gallows, Erik still blamed me for his death, which took place in that last, final confrontation."

"And you're saying . . . ?"

"While the same blood flowed in their veins, the brothers were enough different that I'm not convinced Erik would have the hate to have killed Portia Regan. He reserved his hate for me. That's why he lured me up here with the ghost sightings facade."

"Don't forget the cat drownings—rather brutal, that."

"I'll give you that, but still . . ."

"You don't think he killed Portia Regan."

"At this point, I have to defer to what you think, and what the mayor and others feel they should do, to determine the end of this. I know I'm in the minority on this, and I don't have any evidence that someone else is involved. Just a feeling."

"Yes, your killer profiles. Well, as far as I'm concerned, John, the case is closed. And I know the others feel as I do."

"Yes. And Penny and I will be leaving Sunday. But all the same, Bruce, I'd like you to do one thing, assuming *Hamlet* goes on tomorrow night."

"Yes?"

"Station O'Reilly and Ramsdell near the theater. Ask Clive to post his deputies in and around the theater. Just in case."

Chapter Twenty-Two

Saturday Morning, June 28

"That was the mayor," John Darnell said. "He's bringing his wife to breakfast this morning."

"Good. She's been so attentive to me here. Motherly, you know. I'm going to miss her."

"I think he regards it as sort of preliminary farewell."

"No big farewell dinner tonight?"

He smiled. "One never knows. Maybe we'll just have one of our own up here in our room. Champagne . . ."

"You know I don't drink spirits right now, John."

". . . I was going to add, and sarsaparilla for you."

Penny took a chair and watched Darnell put the finishing touches on a tie, and pull on a light coat. "Can you believe," she mused, "it's less than eight weeks now until we have our own son or daughter?"

"You've done so well here. And today? How do you feel this morning?"

"I'm hungry. I sometimes think I should say, *we're* hungry."

"Eating for two. The old expression."

She laughed. "And gaining a ton of weight in the process. Are you ready now?"

"Let's go."

They took the stairs down to the lobby and strolled across to the dining room, which was already bustling with tourists up and about, ready for their day of sightseeing and shopping, Darnell thought, before the play that night. With that thought, he looked at Penny, and said, "If they put on the play, are you sure you want to attend?"

She sniffed. "Of course, I do. This is the big night. You've got your criminal. John Barrymore's last night here. Yes, I'm going." She frowned at him. "Aren't you?"

"Oh, I'll be there. Maybe not in my seat. I expect to be prowling around the grounds or the theater. Oh—there's the mayor. He can tell us if the plans are on."

Mayor Aylmer walked up vigorously with his wife Kimberley on his arm. She and Penny embraced quickly while John and the mayor shook hands. As the host took them to their table, Aylmer spoke up at once with spirit. "The play's on, John. Flint and Latimer both approved it. Flint said Stanford Vance will take Berg's place—that is, Baldrik's—as Guildenstern."

"He and Willa Skelton . . ." Penny began.

"Yes," Kimberley Aylmer said. "A nice couple. Maybe this will help him out, get him some better roles."

"It's an ill wind . . ." Aylmer said, letting it dangle, as they reached their table.

After they had taken seats and the waiter had filled their cups with steaming coffee, Aylmer beamed at the Darnells with an obvious glow of contentment spread across his smiling face. "Now, here's the big news—I called the aides to the Prince of Wales last night, gave them the news about Baldrik. They said the Prince was waiting for that, and ordered his private car hooked on to the train immediately. He's anxious to see John Barrymore in *Hamlet*. We're picking him up at the station at three p.m. And we have the best suite arranged for him in our finest hotel."

"Not this one?" Penny looked disappointed. "I think this one is pretty fine."

The mayor nodded. "He wanted as much anonymity as he

could get, and he'll return to London tonight by train after the play."

Darnell sat silently, scowling. He emptied his coffee cup and motioned to the waiter for more.

"You look glum, John," Aylmer said. "This is a coup. You'll get to sit in the same audience as the Prince watching one of the greatest American actors."

"I doubt that I'll be watching much of it, Blake." His scowl did not lift. "I'll have things to do."

"Still expecting that elusive . . ." Aylmer lowered his voice, ". . . unknown killer? Sure he isn't another ghost, John?"

"The facts and my ideas, Blake, are quite contradictory. I'm sure that Erik Baldrik is dead. But nevertheless I feel that the Prince could be in danger tonight. It's an unease."

"But the words 'sure' and 'could be'—they don't go together, do they John?" Kimberley Aylmer said.

"You're right. There's nothing certain I can point to. I just feel that the curtain hasn't fallen yet on the last act of this ghostly little drama. And it may not end until the curtain comes down on the last act of *Hamlet* tonight."

John Barrymore pulled Felicia Baron close to him on the sofa and refilled their glasses with champagne. "Happy?" he asked.

"Happy to be with you, yes. Happy you're going to do *Hamlet* tonight. Not happy you're leaving tomorrow." Her head rested easily in the crook of his arm and her gaze searched his face.

Barrymore leaned down and touched her lips with his. "Then come with me. See New York. I know everybody there. You can act on the New York stage."

"You know I'd love it. But—well, my plan was always to go on the stage in London. Maybe with Shaw, in one of his."

He sighed. "Things change. This week has changed me. Finding you here."

"You'll be back in England soon. I know it."

"And we've been down that road." He looked into her green eyes, sparkling in the morning sunrays slanting through his windows. He felt a peace with her, just being with her, but also a gnawing in the pit of his stomach with the thought of leaving her the next day, perhaps forever. He finished his glass and refilled it. "Drink up," he said. "The day awaits us."

She laughed. "John, sometimes I think you talk like Shakespeare writes your lines. And don't you think you've had enough to drink? Tonight's the big play."

Barrymore smiled. "It'll wear off by then. Besides, a little glow doesn't always do harm—up there on the stage."

Rex Flint felt he had his hands full as never before in his career as director at the Shakespeare Memorial Theater. Hard enough, that it was the sesquicentennial festival, a hundred-and-fifty years since David Garrick first dreamed up the festival idea all those years ago in 1769. He wondered how Garrick coped with that first festival. He knew it was comprehensive, with an oratorio, an ode by Garrick, even a minuet danced by his wife.

But Flint felt he had problems Garrick never had—two murders, a dead actor who was shown to be a murderer, someone he must replace in the role of Guildenstern. A wife he must still persuade that he did not kill Portia Regan and also that his affair with the actress had been of no meaning whatsoever. Chief Inspector Howard and ghost-hunter Darnell breathing down his neck, still probing about Portia's death. And, finally, a famous American actor, John Barrymore, about to go on his stage in just six hours in the Stratford play of the year—*Hamlet*. Hearing the knock on his door, he gulped the last of the scotch he'd sipped from the water glass, and returned the bottle and glass to his bottom desk drawer where he liked keeping them—for times like this. The knock would be Stanford Vance.

"Come," he said, and Vance entered, carefully closing the door behind him and taking a seat opposite Flint, who sat behind his desk, in the long-established routine the director expected of his actors and actresses.

"Can you do it?" Flint eyed Vance across his desk.

"Guildenstern? Of course. When you told me about it last night, I reviewed the script again and marked all the lines. But I've known them for months, wanted to play one of them. I love the Rosencrantz, Guildenstern thing! What a pair!"

"You'll be working closely with Perkins. Any problem there?"

"No. I know that story. He's just young and impressionable."

"And you're not?"

Vance laughed. "Not quite so."

Flint sighed. Dealing with actors was like being a doctor, treating this ill or that, sometimes even of the personality or psyche. "All right. Now, when you come on stage in your first scene, you may hear a little buzz in the audience. You know, they realize Berg is dead and you're his replacement. Just some whispering and ogling. Don't let that bother you."

"I understand." Vance stood and said, "That's it, then?"

"That's it—*Guildenstern.*"

Vance laughed again as he left the office. Flint watched him go and checked his watch. He'd promised to go home for lunch today to talk with his wife. But convincing Glenna to trust him again might not be so easy as counseling an actor. Not when he had to continue to lie to her about how he'd felt about Portia, and about what went on those last few nights.

★ ★ ★ ★ ★

Citizens of Stratford-upon-Avon spoke to each other of the death of Erik Berg the night before in either hushed or excited tones, depending upon their personalities, and speculated on the effect it would all have on the play that night. Anne Burghe heard the rumblings as she took care of her daily chores about town and conducted one short tour of the monuments and homes where tourists could bask in the atmosphere of Shakespeare before the evening's event. The few books in town about the Barrymores or acting families of America, imported by booksellers from London, had long been sold out.

Anne stopped by and talked with Penny Darnell in her room, where Penny relaxed and read, preparatory for the long play that night. "It's the sitting bothers me," Penny said, "in my condition. I'll probably have to take an extra intermission or two for myself." Penny had arranged to hold a seat for Anne, who indicated, holding back some information from her, that she'd be a bit late. No need to concern anyone unnecessarily, she thought.

In her route back to her home in the early evening, she saw Professor Darnell and the chief inspector strolling about the grounds of the theater, talking. Why they still showed that strong an interest in the area seemed odd. After all, hadn't the killer been caught—and himself killed?

After a cold supper that night, she cleared off her dining room table and prepared for her visitor. She laid out the pages of the play script one by one on the surface of the otherwise bare table, first page at the lower left side of the table. All was in readiness. In the growing dusk, and as a last thought, with a small smile on her face, she lit two tapers on the top of the sideboard against the wall. Would the atmosphere make a difference in the result? Practically, not—but she felt both excited and romantic, in the broad sense of the word, as she waited for her own adventure, and wanted it to be memorable. An evening that could create a very different life for herself and for her daughter, Anna Maria.

Chapter Twenty-Three

Saturday Evening, June 28

The town of Stratford-upon-Avon seemed to light up with the streetlamps as dusk set in and the hour of the presentation of *Hamlet* approached. Some tourists enjoyed their meals before the theater, while others took liquid refreshment only, planning on a late supper following the play. The townspeople were busy serving the tourists and play-goers, and scheming to find a way to attend the play themselves. Penny Darnell took all this in, and seemed to feel the vibrations of excitement emanating from people in inns, stores, and restaurants as she walked toward the Shakespeare Theater at just before seven p.m., to be early. Darnell had gone ahead to meet with Chief Howard, and she knew the importance of it, but missed him by her side.

As she entered the theater shortly, she cheered up seeing the familiar faces of Mayor and Kimberley Aylmer. Sergeant Catherine O'Reilly, in uniform, evidently ready for her duty that night in the theater, smiled as she approached.

"Hello, Catherine," Penny said, and impulsively took her in her arms in an embrace. "Are you expecting any trouble tonight?"

O'Reilly smiled. "Not me, personally, Penny, but—well, your husband has this bee in his bonnet."

"I know. He said he's just not sure it's over—even with young Baldrik dead."

"We're taking all precautions. The chief and Constable Clive are placing men outside right now. And John's there with them."

"Will you be able to see the play?"

"I'll be at the stage door at first. Later I can see some of it from here, keeping an eye out for anything suspicious. We have another reason to be at our best and on our guard tonight."

"The Prince."

The Sergeant nodded. "I've never seen him up close. This will be a great chance to do that." She pointed toward the front doors. "He'll come right through those doors about eight, take the stairs up to the next level and to his special front box. By then, I'll be coming back to the lobby."

"Well . . . I'll find my seat, now. I'll see you later on."

As Penny found her seat in the second row, center, she laid her jacket on the aisle seat next to her, one reserved for Anne Burghe. The mayor's wife was on her right and they engaged in conversation while the mayor studied the program. Excitement rippled through the audience in little waves as people took their seats, met friends, and began discussing the play. The word had begun to circulate also that the Prince of Wales would be there, and many already gazed up at the front box, watching, wanting, as Penny could imagine, to be among the first to see him arrive.

The orchestra struck up a light tune, which added to the gaiety of the evening, although Penny knew from the performance of *Macbeth* that it was prepared with more somber selections, suitable to enhance the gravity of the play. As she sat, very comfortable at the moment, hands resting contentedly on her mid-section, her mind drifted slowly back to London, to their flat, and to that now delicate little room opposite theirs on the second floor where in just weeks the occupant would be a new baby boy or girl with the last name of Darnell.

She wished once more, as she had many times, that her

father and mother, and John's father and mother, could be alive for the event. But, at least she and John would name the newborn by combining something of each family name, for a remembrance.

From the edge of the riverbank, Darnell stood with the chief as they watched people pour into the theater, most walking from the village inns and hotels, some being dropped off from cars in front of the theater. "The last night, Chief," Darnell said. "Then back to London for all of us."

"Yes, the last one—and I hope an uneventful one."

Darnell clicked open his watchcase. "It's almost seven. Are all your men in place?"

Chief Howard nodded. "A block apart, in a loose rectangle about the theater. Our car will bring the Prince to the front entrance at eight. Flint won't begin the play, of course, until the Prince is seated. Constable Clive's up at the Prince's box, and he'll open the box door for the Prince and his companion." He smiled. "A very lovely young lady, I might add."

"What will you do?"

"I'll make rounds of my men again. Don't worry, John—everything's covered. When the car arrives, my sergeant will lead the Prince and the lady up the stairs, to the box, myself following them, then their aide. Will you watch the play?"

Darnell scowled. "I doubt that. I have some ideas—in fact, I'm going down there now. I want to be positioned early."

Anne Burghe's heart jumped when she heard the knock on the door at exactly seven p.m. He was right on time, yet the thrill of it, the anticipation, brought her to a state of excitement unusual in her quiet life. She hurried to the front door and swung it open.

He entered slowly, looking about the room as if expecting someone to be there. "You're alone?" He walked further into the room and noticed the loose pages lying on the dining room table.

"Of course I'm alone." She tried to be steady, but felt a tremble in her voice. Anxiously, she took a place by his side at the table, when he walked to it.

Satisfied no one was there, he dropped a folder he'd brought onto a nearby chair and bent over the table, eyes wide, studying the pages of the script, but not touching them. "*Hamlet.*" He said the one word, but it carried much meaning for Anne Burghe.

She responded in kind. "*Shakespeare.*"

The man took a large magnifying glass from his coat pocket and examined each page through it, inspecting particularly the signature or initials that appeared on each page.

He turned to her. "No one else knows about this? *No one?*"

"Not a soul. And I haven't mentioned you, as you asked."

He scowled. "The professor? You've spent time with them."

She shook her head. "I was going to ask him about this, but he was occupied. My time there was mostly with his wife."

The man's attitude changed subtly and he moved closer to her. He reached out and touched her hair, smoothed it back, then stroked her cheek. "It's been a long time, Anne."

She put her hands on his chest, between them, holding him back. "I—I don't know. It's the script I want—"

By this time both of his large hands were on her shoulders, then caressing her neck, then pressing in on her throat, and she suddenly could not speak, could not breathe, and her eyes seemed to expand to twice their size as she stared at his now-contorted face, unbelieving that this was happening. She beat on his chest with her hands, but soon her eyes rolled back, her head fell to one side, and her arms dangled loosely. Her world went black.

The man allowed her body to drop to the floor, stared at it for a moment, then turned quickly to the folder he had brought with him. He opened it and stepped back to the table. He picked up the script pages, one by one, and placed the delicate sheets in the folder, one on top of the other, swiftly but carefully, not to tear or wrinkle any of them.

When he had them all secured, he closed the folder and re-placed a rubber band about it for security. He glanced at the lifeless-looking body on the floor and retraced his steps to the front door. He opened it slightly, looked out both ways into the now-darkened street, grateful that the nearest street lamp was several doors from the house. He pulled down his hat and turned up his coat collar, quickly stepped out through the front doorway, and pulled the door closed behind him.

Keeping his head down, he walked along the short brick path to the street and crossed it diagonally, striding briskly away from Anne Burghe's house. Although he passed a few other pedestrians, they were laughing and talking and took no notice of him. Two streets away, he slowed his pace as he reached his parked car. He stepped into it and started the engine. As he drove off, his dark thoughts swirled . . . *Only one more thing to do now—one more score to settle.*

On a deserted side street, he pulled in to a curb. With the engine still running, he took clothing articles from the back seat and, after removing his outer coat and hat, pulled them on, along with a stage beard. *A half-hour to go—perfect.* He drove to the theater, and, as a car pulled away from the curb across the street, he parked, took a deep breath, and stepped out.

★ ★ ★ ★ ★

Inside the Memorial Theater, conversations in the audience reached ever higher levels, as anticipation built toward the imminent arrival of the Prince of Wales and the beginning of the play. Behind the curtain, in the wings to the left of the stage, Rex Flint spoke to his principal cast members who formed a loose circle about him.

"Yes, the Prince will be here, and I'm going out to the lobby now to be part of his welcoming. But don't let his presence affect your performance. Of course, do your best—but don't be overly nervous, don't play to the Prince's box, and for God's sake, don't overact. Remember your roles, and stay within them, within character. You can't all be Hamlets."

They laughed lightly at that and looked at John Barrymore, who smiled back and nodded. Across from him, Felicia Baron looked into his eyes, and when his gaze found hers, smiled.

"So," Flint said, "you know who does what. I'll be back here as soon as we greet the Prince and he goes to his box. When he's seated, we begin. And let's give him a night to remember!"

He left the wings and by a circuitous route backstage wound his way to the front of the theater, passing Sergeant O'Reilly on his way and nodding at her. He reached the front door of the lobby just as the police car drove up. Chief Howard walked to the car, opened the door, and the Prince of Wales and a young woman stepped out. Sergeant Ramsdell, who had driven the car, hurried around it and led the way up to the theater, the chief behind the Prince. Reaching Flint, Chief Howard said, "Allow me to present the play's Director, Your Highness—Mr. Rex Flint."

The Prince said, "Charmed. I know I'll enjoy your play." His companion nodded and smiled. Flint stepped to one side and the procession went on into the lobby. He followed but stayed in the lobby as the others continued up the stairs, Ramsdell in front, the Prince and the lady, Howard, then the aide, walking toward the constable who stood near the Prince's box, beaming.

A lone usher in the lobby stood with Flint, watching the entourage go up the stairs. Later, the young man would describe what happened in the next minute as *"All hell breaking loose."* When the group reached the landing, a man in actor's garb jumped out from an alcove—*"From nowhere,"* in the usher's words—and launched himself at Chief Howard, striking him on the head with a metal pipe. The chief fell hard.

Dropping the pipe, the man next drew out a long knife whose blade flashed in the light. The Prince pushed his lady companion behind him, and turned toward the oncoming assailant.

The young Prince's aide rushed forward but stumbled over Howard. It appeared the assailant would reach the Prince until, in seconds, a closet door, standing ajar opposite the Prince, flew open, and John Darnell lunged into the corridor and charged the attacker. The force of their combined assaults threw them both to the floor, grappling and rolling over in a grim struggle.

In moments, they reached the edge of the stairs, and at once began rolling down it, tumbling one over the other, locked in each other's grasp, falling down all the way, bumping down the steps. Darnell focused on keeping the blade of the knife away from his throat, gripping the man's right wrist tightly. As they reached the bottom of the stairs, Darnell took the worst of the fall, underneath the other, and cracked his head on the hard edge of the banister post at the base of the stairs.

Stunned, Darnell came close to losing his consciousness but was aware through a red glow that the attacker had jumped up and run toward Rex Flint, grabbing him, forcing him along with the threat of his knife at the man's throat, running with him across the lobby and out of the theater and across the street. The usher ran over to Darnell and lifted up his head. "Sir, sir!" he said. "Are you all right?" Darnell tried to get his voice going, shook his head, getting out the words, "I don't know."

Just then, Sergeant Ramsdell reached the landing where Darnell had fallen. Not stopping, Ramsdell ran past him to the door and looked out as a car roared away. He ran back to Darnell, who was now sitting up and shaking his head.

By that time, the constable also had run down the stairs. He shouted, *"After him!"*

The sergeant answered, "They left in a car, but I got the plate number—four-eight-nine."

Darnell brought himself to a standing position against the wall and stared at the constable. "The Prince is all right?"

Constable Clive said, "Thanks to you, yes, sir. He's safe in his box. He asked your name. The aide's there. But the man, actor, whoever the hell he was—he's got Rex Flint in that car."

Darnell rubbed his head. "Get a car around front."

"There's one there," the sergeant said. "The one I brought the Prince in. I have the keys."

"Good! Give them to me. Sergeant, see to Chief Howard. Constable, guard the Prince. Stay by that door to his box. The Prince's safety is paramount. There could be others in on this."

Keys in hand, Darnell ran to the front door. Outside he tumbled into the car, started it, and drove off. As he reached the corner, he saw a car in the distance he thought could be it.

Sam McCarver

★ ★ ★ ★ ★

Constable Clive and Ramsdell raced back up the stairs and found Chief Howard reaching a sitting position and rubbing his head. Ramsdell asked, "Are you all right?"

"My head . . . what a blow!"

Clive said, "I'll guard the door to the Prince's box. Come over, if you're able." Clive ran on and positioned himself outside the door, which was slightly open.

Howard pulled himself up by the railing and tested his balance. He felt dizzy, his ears were ringing, and he could feel a painful lump forming on the back of his head. *Too old for this!* he thought. *This has to be the last time.*

He walked slowly, holding the rail, crossing the mezzanine landing toward the constable. When he reached the door, he again sank down to the floor against the wall. He heard loud applause coming from the audience. He and Clive glanced into the box through the doorway. The Prince and his companion were standing and waving to the audience. When the Prince took his seat, the applause began to die down. The Prince looked over his shoulder at Clive. The constable said softly but urgently, "Everything's under control, Your Highness. I'll be outside here. The play—I don't know—might be late. The man took the director hostage."

After Clive closed the door, Howard said, "We have to tell someone down there—Flint's assistant—about this. No one knows what's happened. The play can't go on—not yet. Not with all this."

The usher who had been in the lobby hurried up to them, panting. "I told Danny Marek what happened. The actors all heard it, too. And I told your sergeant—oh, here she comes."

Sergeant O'Reilly ran across the mezzanine from the stairs. "My God! Chief, are you all right?"

"I guess I'll live through it." He rubbed his head.

206

The usher said, "Danny's going to make an announce-ment."

The chief looked down the hall. "There are other boxes here. We could go into one and listen."

Sergeant O'Reilly ran to the nearest box, rapped on the door, and stepped inside. In a moment, she came out, leaving the door open, and came back to the chief. "Let's go in, Chief. Then I have to see Penny, and also Mrs. Flint, if she's here. They shouldn't hear the news that way. I'll be back."

The usher helped Chief Howard into the box where he took an empty seat next to the two occupants, the owner of the Anne Hathaway Inn and his daughter. The usher stood by. As the chief looked down into the audience, he saw O'Reilly run up the aisle. She found Penny Darnell and spoke to her, then asked a question of the mayor, who shook his head negatively. O'Reilly and Penny hurried back up the aisle together, toward the lobby.

Within minutes, the two women had come upstairs and joined Chief Howard in the box. Sergeant O'Reilly told the chief, "Mrs. Flint isn't here. We'll have to call her at home."

Penny urged him, "Is John all right? Tell me everything that happened. *Please, Bruce!*"

Howard knew he had to reassure her. "John's armed," he said. "I'm certain no harm will come to him."

With a stunned look on her face, Penny sat down in a chair. O'Reilly stood next to her, and put an arm around her shoulders.

Danny Marek came out on the stage and spoke. "Due to unusual circumstances, our play will be delayed. We can't say how long, and we ask for your patience." He looked up at the Prince of Wales, who nodded. "We hope the play will begin soon. Meanwhile, Mr. John Barrymore has graciously volun-

207

teered to come out on stage and entertain you. I'm sure you'll enjoy that."

As Chief Howard listened, he also reflected on what he'd told Penny. He knew Darnell was anything but safe from harm—and that John's worst fears that a second vicious killer was at large and could strike again had been true, from the very beginning.

Chapter Twenty-Four

Saturday Night, June 28

John Barrymore faced Danny Marek as he stepped back behind the curtain and into the wings. "I'll need some assistance, Danny. We don't know how long this will take. I can't just talk to them for hours. They'll get bored."

"I don't think so . . . but what do you suggest?"

"Give me Felicia Baron. She played Lady Macbeth, and tonight she's Ophelia. We'll do some short scenes from each play as sort of a—well, a review and a preview."

"All right. Good." He looked over at a group of actors and actresses, talking, and called, "Felicia . . ."

She walked over to them. Marek nodded at Barrymore, who explained his idea to her quickly.

"I don't know . . ."

"Come on, Felicia—a chance for the spotlight. An actor never turns that down. Besides, we have to do something while someone tries to bring back old Rex. And the Prince of Wales is out there. Your own royalty."

She smiled, "All right, John. But you lead. You decide what we're to do. I'll just follow. You're the star, you know."

Barrymore put his arm around her shoulders and walked toward the center of the stage. "After this night, my dear, *you'll* be a star. Special performances for the Prince of Wales? You'll be in the *London Times* tomorrow." He kissed her lightly on the lips as they reached the gap where the curtains came together. "It's a parting gift from me to you, Felicia. *Instant fame!*"

209

* * * * *

Darnell swerved from one road to the next, speeding up now in the lighter traffic, keeping an eye on the car over two blocks ahead of him. It had raced with abandon, recklessly, through the city streets, almost colliding with other cars and coming close to striking a pedestrian. Darnell had driven more cautiously, and the pain in his head, now also down into his shoulders, impeded his driving. *He had to keep up with the car!* But the city street lamps no longer stood at each intersection, and the road was only dirt now, unpaved. Dust thrown up by the roaring car ahead obscured his vision, and he could hardly see the car.

Suddenly the car ahead was no longer visible. He put on the brakes and the car skidded to a stop. He looked back and saw a cloud of dust going up a side road to a house set back from the road. He backed up and turned into the road, following the other car. When he reached the house, he saw the car parked, front doors both open, apparently abandoned quickly. He jumped out, pulled his .38 special revolver from his pocket, ran up on a porch to the front door, and pushed the door open.

On the far side of the room, a desperate-looking man still in his actor's outer clothing but with the stage beard removed, held Rex Flint in his grasp as a shield in front of his own body, with a knife to the director's throat. The man yelled, *"Stop! Or this man dies."*

Darnell held his revolver close to his side at an angle not visible to the assailant. *How could he get off a shot without endangering Flint?* "Don't do anything foolish," Darnell called to him across the room. *Got to get him talking, distracted, then maybe . . .* He said, "Why are you doing this? If you surrender, no harm will come to you."

"No harm? You don't know the harm that has *already* come to me."

"The man's crazy," Flint yelled. "It's Victor Blount."

Darnell blinked at that. Yes, it was the bookstore owner. But why . . . ?

"Tell me about it, Mr. Blount. Tell me your complaints. We can look into them."

"Hah! You want to know? Flint, here. He was the first. He cut me to pieces—cut my lines, my parts, then let me go as an actor two years ago. Said I drank too much and fumbled my lines. Then Portia—sweet Portia—turned her back on me and took up with him. And I had to find a new way to live, with my bookstore."

"You killed Portia," Darnell said, then regretted it, not wanting to stress the man's criminality.

But Blount answered readily. "Yes, I killed her. It felt good to press my hands around her neck and squeeze the life out of her. The watchman—he was a mere nuisance. Wanted money to keep quiet. Well, I quieted him. And Flint would have got his tonight, too, if the damn Prince hadn't come. I couldn't resist that target."

"But why? Why Flint? Why the Prince?"

"To ruin Flint's precious festival forever. To get even with these unfeeling, self-centered . . ." His voice caught and he faltered in his speech. Perspiration glistened on his forehead.

Darnell heard a noise, a roaring, outside, and realized another car was rushing up the road toward the house. Blount shifted his gaze to the front windows. The car skidded to a halt on the dirt road. And the sound of a second car could now be heard, also racing to the house on the road.

Chief Inspector Howard and Sandy MacDougall burst through the open front door, and pulled up, taking in the scene. "It's over," Howard said. "Give it up. You'll be surrounded in a minute."

The second car stopped and Darnell heard new sounds of

more running footsteps, up the wooden steps and across the porch. Howard turned toward the door and held up a hand to say stop as Sergeant O'Reilly and Sergeant Ramsdell rushed in. At his signal, they stood as if glued to the spot, eyes wide, looking from one to the other of those in the room.

"Burghe had to die," Blount went on. "She had something I wanted, and expected *me* to help her with it, after she turned me out last year. Now I have it, it's mine—and I put her down."

Anne Burghe! Darnell looked at the chief, who nodded, but with his arm straight down at his side, he also moved his right hand in a slicing motion, left to right. Darnell frowned. What was the chief trying to say? Don't pursue it?

"It's no use, Blount," Howard said. "Come quietly, and you'll have the justice of the courts. English justice."

"Hah! I'll take my own . . ." Blount pushed Flint down on the floor, and Darnell quickly brought his .38 up, leveled at him, but the man viciously drew the flashing bright blade of the knife across his own throat, deeply, blood spurting out from the obvious severing of his jugular vein, and he fell on top of Flint, blood running over the director and the floor. Flint disentangled himself, pulled himself up, and backed away, wiping blood from his face with his arm. Blount said nothing else, nor could he. His eyes closed, his face grimaced with death throes, and his body abruptly went totally limp.

Darnell stared at the body, then turned to Howard. "Anne Burghe—you were trying to tell me something. What is it?"

The chief nodded. "She's going to be all right, John. He tried to strangle her, but she fainted. She was able to get help from a neighbor; they took her to Doctor Geary's home, and he got a message through to Constable Clive at the theater. That's how we knew to come here. Fortunately, Sandy's car was near. Then my sergeants followed along as soon as they could."

"And Clive?"

"He's still guarding the Prince. The Prince is safe."

"The Prince! The play! My God!" Flint looked anxiously about the room. "I have to get back."

Howard said to Ramsdell, "Sergeant, get the director back there as soon as you can."

Ramsdell and Flint ran out, and in moments Darnell heard the car start and roar off. He looked at Howard. "What else? Blount said he got something from Anne." He glanced at Blount's body, then looked back. "What was it?"

Howard turned to O'Reilly. "Catherine?"

She nodded. "When word came from the doctor's office, Art and I took a car there to see her. She told us she owned a valuable script, and that Blount strangled her and stole it. She gave us the directions to his house."

"Where's the script now?" Darnell took in Howard and O'Reilly in a glance. "It has to be here . . . oh, I know, it must be in his car."

Darnell whirled and ran out to Blount's car, followed by MacDougall. Howard and O'Reilly remained in the house, talking.

At the car, Darnell glanced in the front seat then saw the brown folder in the back seat. He reached in and took it. He looked at MacDougall for the first time. "You're getting quite a story, aren't you Sandy? Write the headline yet?"

"The *Times* will have to put in several headlines to cover *this* story. Ghosts, conspiracy, theft, revenge, murder!"

Darnell walked back into the house without opening the folder. "Chief," he said, "I'd like to return this to Anne myself. Is she still at the doctor's house?"

O'Reilly said, "She was when we left. He wanted to observe her for a while. She was resting."

Howard nodded. "You two take that car and go. See her, and set her mind at peace. Then get Doctor Geary out here to pronounce this man dead, and Ramsdell and a couple of Clive's men to come and take the body. MacDougall and I will stay here."

Darnell looked down at Blount's body, still draped in an old Shakespearian costume, probably one stolen from the theater, now red with his own blood. "He was once an actor," Darnell said. "His last scene may have been his best."

When Rex Flint reached the theater and had washed his face and pulled on a clean jacket in his office, he hurried down the aisle toward the stage, abandoning his usual practice of stepping out on stage from behind a curtain. No time for formalities.

John Barrymore saw him coming and declaimed, "Here comes our director, Mr. Rex Flint!"

All eyes turned toward Flint, who strode quickly down the aisle, up the steps on the left, and out onto the stage. He shook hands with Barrymore and Felicia Baron amid applause.

Turning to the audience he said, "First, let me thank you all for your patience. The play will go on!" He looked up to the box where the Prince of Wales smiled and nodded. "Then let us all thank Mr. Barrymore and Miss Felicia Baron for their entertainment of you during this delay." The applause continued for a minute or two while Barrymore and Felicia bowed, then turned and stepped through the connecting gap of the curtains.

Flint went on. "Now, with a brief—very brief—orchestral interlude, we will bring you, just as quickly as possible, our production of William Shakespeare's *Hamlet*, with the famous American actor you already have come to know in the starring role—Mr. John Barrymore." Flint nodded at the orchestra leader, who struck up a lively melody, and he stepped through the curtain gap, following in the steps of Barrymore and Felicia.

Inside the curtain, he looked around the stage at the assembled cast. He pulled out his watch. "Ten to nine. We begin the play at nine. Are you ready?" He heard the word "Yes" from all. "Then get ready, into your positions. Where are my soldiers for scene one, Bernardo and Francisco?"

Two men stepped forward. "Bernardo here," one said, and "Francisco," said the other. "We're ready, Rex."

"Then take your posts. The curtain goes up in eight minutes now." As if in acknowledgment of his command, the orchestra shifted to a more somber piece, an introduction to Shakespeare's tragedy, *Hamlet.*

Darnell handed the folder to Anne Burghe, who still rested on the doctor's sofa, but now alone. Ramsdell had stopped there and taken the doctor in a car with two of Clive's deputies, heading to Blount's place to deal with the body.

Sergeant O'Reilly said to Anne, "If there's anything you need, let me know. Would you like some water?"

Anne Burghe nodded. "Yes, if you wouldn't mind. I'm suddenly very thirsty."

O'Reilly left the room to go into the doctor's kitchen. Anne watched her leave.

"I wanted to ask you, Professor, privately . . ." She held up the folder. "This contains what I wanted to show you."

"I, ah, I'm sorry I never had the time—*took* the time."

"I understand that. But what I want now is that you look at it, examine it, and give me your best opinion. Obviously, Victor—that's Blount, you know—thought it was valuable

215

enough to kill for. Of course, he hated me, too, since we broke up."

"Shall I open it and examine it now?"

"Please. You could spread the pages out on the doctor's dining room table. That's what I do."

Sergeant O'Reilly brought in a glass of water, helped Anne into more of a sitting position, and handed her the glass. As Anne sipped the water, the sergeant moved to the side of Darnell, who had stepped over to the table with the folder.

Darnell removed the only object on the table, a white lace cloth, and put it to one side. He opened the folder and took the pages of the script out one by one, placing them in even rows in order on the table. Eight pages. He scanned them quickly. The last seven pages initialed at the bottom, *"W.S."* The first page, signed in full at the top, *"Wm. Shakespeare."* He looked quickly at Anne.

She nodded and said, "Look at them closely before you say anything."

Darnell bent over the table, studying the delicate and parchment-like sheets, noticing the faintness of the ink in many spots. One thing was clear—these were the first eight pages of a script of *Hamlet* by someone who signed his name, *"Shakespeare."*

The reading that he'd done at night on Shakespeare in their room at the Anne Hathaway Inn crept back into his mind, along with what he remembered from his study of the history of the town and its former inhabitants associated with the plays and the festivals. He recalled his previous studies of Shakespeare at Oxford and Cambridge. All this passed quickly through his mind. He shook his head. One thing that had been drilled into all of them in college, as students, one affirmation about which there was complete unanimity in all the treatises he'd ever examined was—*there were no scripts of*

Shakespeare's plays in his own hand!

Background was what Darnell needed first. He turned to Anne Burghe. "If you're up to it, Anne, I want you to tell me how you acquired these pages. Tell me anything that could be relevant." He took a straight chair from the dining room table to the sofa and sat near her. "What you know about those eight sheets of paper could be very important."

Chapter Twenty-five

Saturday Night, June 28

Anne Burghe said, "I've held back until you could see the script yourself. But I'll tell you everything now." She paused, looking at John Darnell. Sergeant O'Reilly sat at the table.

"Our family," Anne said, "has lived in Stratford-upon-Avon for many generations. I told Penny something about them. My mother spoke to me of my great-grandmother, Anna Maria de Burghe Ireland. Her father was an early settler here. I never knew her, she died before my time, but I named my daughter after her. I'm sure the trunk in my attic, where I found the script, was Anna Maria's. The other relics indicated that. The script was boxed, and unusually well-preserved all those years. I hadn't looked into the trunk since I was a child, until this year."

"Your great-grandmother, the original Anna Maria—what was her father's name?"

"William Henry Ireland. His father was Samuel Ireland. She kept her maiden name. Samuel was already well-settled here in the late 1700's—maybe even born here, I don't know—when William settled down here with him at age eighteen, perhaps after some schooling elsewhere. That's where the records seem to begin.

"Anyway, his father, Samuel, was obsessed with Shakespeare and wanted memorabilia from Shakespeare's days. William, who would have been my great-great-grandfather, tried to accommodate his father." She paused. "And this is where it gets embarrassing, and also what bothered me about the script. I wanted to know it was genuine, for its value. But William—well, there's simply no other way to say it . . . he was a *forger*."

Darnell nodded, and smiled. "I knew that much, Anne. I've read about him over this past week in a dusty old work on the town and its history that I bought at Blount's bookstore."

Anne cringed at Blount's name. "One thing," she said, "if there's anything to be proud of amid all the embarrassment and shame—William was at least a master-forger. He began to forge documents regarding Shakespeare himself, for his father, and to give them to him as presents. Forged mortgages, notes, and letters. He got special ancient ink that would turn brown and look authentic. He used parchment, made seals and affixed them."

"And you think he may have forged these script pages?"

"Exactly. I couldn't ignore his entire lifestyle. Although I hoped—and wished—it was truly Shakespeare's writing." She paused and smiled a bit. "William, at only nineteen, even went on to forge a note from Queen Elizabeth to Shakespeare. And then he wrote a play he attributed to Shakespeare, and called it *Vortigern*." She laughed. "It was awful! People walked out of the theater, and it played only one pitiful performance."

"But I understand he went on with forgeries a long time."

"Yes, the notes I have show he did it for years. His first drafts of his memoirs discuss his fraudulent works. His papers, all the forgeries, were taken on by the Shakespeare Memorial Library in Birmingham, and it and all its contents were totally destroyed by fire in 1879." She gestured toward the pages on the table. "Those pages—whether they're Shakespeare's priceless writings or worthless forgeries—are all that's left of any possible value among all the family relics old Anna Maria was able to keep from her father's papers in that old trunk."

Sergeant O'Reilly said, "What a story!"

Anne Burghe looked at Darnell with pleading in her eyes. "Tell me, Professor. Genuine or fake? I can take it now, after all I've been through."

Darnell rested a hand on Anne Burghe's shoulder and offered her a handkerchief to blot her tears. "I know how emotional this night has been for you. I'm happy that I can tell you something, Anne, to help set your heart at rest."

As she started to speak, he raised a hand. "No, these pages weren't written by Shakespeare. Of course, that's only my opinion, and we'll have experts look at them. But I must say all the evidence you've given me indicates your ancestor, William Ireland, forged these pages, probably when he was a very young man, in the early 1800's. I imagine your great-grandmother Anna Maria knew the truth. But what she did was more important than telling the bald truth in her notes. *She kept the pages!* And I'll tell you this much, Anne—and I don't have to be an expert to say it. These pages will be worth a great sum to you—"

"—even as forgeries?" Anne's voice showed her eagerness.

"—because any museum will pay a small fortune to get these. Remember, Ireland's other fakeries were destroyed by fire forty years ago. These are the only Ireland Shakespeare imitations left. They're irreplaceable. You and your daughter will be well taken care of by sale of these, Anne. I'll look into it for you in London." He laughed. "And I'm sure experts will pronounce these the only real, genuine, Ireland forgeries in the world!"

By the time Darnell and Sergeant O'Reilly returned to the theater after dropping Anne Burghe off at her house, the play had progressed to act five.

Dr. Geary had returned to his home and office, and with the aid of two deputies, deposited the body of Victor Blount in a room used for that rare purpose, pending transfer next day to the undertaker. Chief Howard and MacDougall had come back from Blount's house also, in the reporter's car, and drove on to the theater as well, after the arrangements had been finished. They arrived at the same time as Darnell and O'Reilly did, and they walked into the theater together.

Howard said, "Catherine, you can take a spot in the lobby in the standing-room area, and see the rest of the play. But keep your eyes open."

"Could there be anything else tonight?"

"I don't think so, but we still have a Prince upstairs. That's responsibility enough."

MacDougall found a table and chair where he could begin writing what Darnell knew he would consider the story of his lifetime. Darnell shook hands with him and said, "Good writing, Sandy. If you have to leave, I'll see you in London."

Darnell came over to Chief Howard and O'Reilly and asked, "How's your head, Bruce? I have to admit mine's still sore."

"The same. I'll need some headache powders tonight."

Darnell smiled. "I'm going to join my wife now and see what's left of this play. Let's have breakfast at the Inn in the morning before we all leave." He passed through the lobby and standing-room area to the aisle, and walked quietly down the aisle in the semi-darkness of the theater. At the second row, he dropped silently into Anne Burghe's aisle seat next to Penny.

She gasped audibly, but whispered, "John . . . thank God you're back."

He spoke low. "It's all over now. Really, this time. And

Anne is fine. I'll tell you all about it after the play."

Penny hooked her arm in his and squeezed it for a moment. Then she leaned her head momentarily against his shoulder, and said, "All's right with the world."

On stage, John Barrymore, as Hamlet, stood with two clowns and Horatio, in a graveyard scene. Hamlet said, *"Let me see,"* and took a skull from a clown. *"Alas! poor Yorick. I knew him, Horatio. A fellow of infinite jest, of most excellent fancy. He hath borne me on his back a thousand times. And now, how abhorred in my imagination it is! My gorge rises at it . . ."*

Penny whispered, "Barrymore has been everything we could expect. He was on stage an hour before the play started, doing scenes with Felicia Baron. I didn't hear much of it. It was nerve-wracking waiting, thinking about you. But then we knew everything was all right when Rex Flint came back. And since then, I've loved it. Barrymore's been the perfect Hamlet."

Darnell put his arm around her shoulders. "The play's almost over, the week is over, and we go home to London tomorrow. What do you think of that, dear?"

"I say, now we can think and talk of nothing but pleasant and wonderful things."

"Of cabbages and kings?"

She smiled. "Yes. And of a beautiful, pink little baby."

When the final curtain fell, and even as the actors were taking their last bows, the Prince's aide came to Darnell's seat and said, "Sir."

Darnell stood. "Yes?"

"The Prince requests your presence in his box."

Darnell turned and looked up at the Prince's box. The Prince of Wales smiled at him and nodded. He gestured lightly to come up.

Darnell told the aide, "Of course, I'll come." He turned to Penny and said, "I'll meet you in the lobby in a short while."

The aide preceded Darnell, leading him up the aisle to the stairs and on up to the Prince's box. Clive still stood there on guard and nodded at Darnell, opening the door as he approached.

Inside, Darnell waited while the door closed behind him.

"Professor Darnell," the Prince of Wales said, "first may I present my companion, Miss Patricia Ardmore."

Darnell said, "Thank you, Your Highness. I'm very pleased to meet you, Miss Ardmore."

The Prince of Wales stepped over to Darnell, who realized for the first time how young the heir to the throne was, just barely in his mid-twenties, and how slight in stature, not over five-foot-eight or so. But royalty always seemed taller.

"Professor Darnell, if we can suspend the formalities for a moment, I want to thank you very personally." He held out a hand which Darnell took in his own. The Prince shook his hand vigorously. "You saved my life, and very possibly that of Miss Ardmore as well. My aide—good lad though he is— would have been no match for that angry, desperate man. I'm leaving tonight, since our plans were to return by train to London immediately after the performance." He smiled. "One gets used to sleeping in Buckingham Palace. And I promised Miss Ardmore's mother I'd return her tonight, even if it's in the wee hours of the morning. But in London, Professor, soon, we'll contact you to offer a more proper recognition of your service."

Darnell said his own thanks for the honor of meeting the Prince and his companion, and let himself out of the box somewhat numb with the effect of close contact with royalty. He nodded at Clive and the aide and walked slowly to the stairs.

Looking down at the lobby, he saw Penny standing there with the mayor and his wife, and his step quickened as he took the stairs down. The talk of London had renewed his anxiety to return there, since his job was done. Much lay ahead in his life and in Penny's, and he wanted to get on with it now. Still, he thought, shaking the hand of the Prince of Wales was something to remember. And it took this trip to Stratford-upon-Avon, two murders, an attempted murder, and an attempted royal assassination to make that possible. Strange world, indeed!

Chapter Twenty-Six

Breakfast at the Inn combined a celebration and a farewell party. The large table took up one side of the restaurant, its occupants seated eight on one side and on the other, one at each end. The mayor and his wife arrived first. Chief Howard, O'Reilly, Ramsdell, Constable Clive, and deputy Ben Carson came in a group. Darnell and Penny came down, joined by Anne Burghe.

John Barrymore and Felicia Baron strolled down from his second floor rooms, arm in arm. Rex Flint, and his red-haired, very subdued wife, Glenna. Danny Marek. Producer Richard Latimer and his wife. And, at Latimer's insistence, the young engaged couple, Willa Skelton, whose father's funeral had taken place the day before, and her fiancé, Stanford Vance.

John Barrymore told Darnell and Penny, "Thank you for saving my play, and the day. I'll be in touch from America, soon."

He and Felicia Baron formed a center of attention after their performances the night before, Barrymore, who would leave that day, seeming to say a misty goodbye to her every time his gaze met hers. Darnell was congratulated by all for saving the Prince's life, and everyone said farewells to Penny and him. Anne Burghe and Kimberley Aylmer hugged Penny, wishing her well.

The table presented the finest foods of the English breakfast table—bacon, sausages, kippers, eggs, crisp toast, juices, fruit, cereal, milk, and pastries. When champagne and other beverages had been poured, Mayor Aylmer stood, cleared his throat, and clinked a glass in front of him with a spoon.

"Friends . . . friends . . . a toast, if you please. Two, in fact. First to Mr. John Barrymore, for his superb performance as Hamlet, making this the greatest Shakespeare festival ever." All raised their glasses. "And second, to Professor John Darnell, who solved our mysteries of ghosts and murders and prevented an attack on our Prince." Applause broke out and glasses were raised again.

Aylmer remained standing. "And let us not forget the women. Felicia Baron, who, with Mr. Barrymore, entertained the audience under difficult circumstances, and Mrs. Penny Darnell, who supported her husband's day and night investigations."

The others again saluted the two women with their glasses and remarks. Aylmer said, "Now, let's have a great breakfast," and sat down. His wife, Kimberley, patted him on the back. "Very nice, dear. Very mayorally."

He smiled. "Mayorally? Is there such a word?"

Darnell leaned over to the mayor on his left and said, "Thank you, again, for that very nice fee. You'll be pleased to know some of it will go for furnishings in our nursery."

Kimberley said to Penny, on Darnell's other side. "Send us word when your baby is born. We want to know about him—or her."

Penny said, "I will. And I'll send you a photograph when we have one taken." She thanked her for all her attentions.

John Darnell glanced about the table as they all occupied themselves with their food. "Penny, take a last look. The good people of Stratford, here to say goodbye."

"Yes, *'Such sweet sorrow.'* "

He laughed. "Shakespeare couldn't say it better."

★ ★ ★ ★ ★

After lunch, driven to the train station by Mayor Aylmer, the Darnells took last looks at the surrounding countryside. After a swift journey on the train back to London where Sung met them at the station, they reached their London flat at dusk.

"Dinner waits," Sung said, as they entered the flat, and his son, Ho San, took their bags upstairs. Penny went on up, also, and stepped immediately into the nursery to look it over. The last touches could be done easily and quickly, and now with great pleasure since nothing stood in the way of their expected delivery date of August 15 but planning and preparation for the event.

Not unexpectedly, but still with some surprise, John Darnell found himself driving Penny to the Royal Hospital six weeks later and five days early on Sunday, August 10. And at almost midnight, the boy they agreed quickly to name Jeffrey Grover, after John's lost brother and Penny's father, gave vent, strongly, in his cries, in his first greeting to the world.

Five days later, when Darnell brought Penny and Jeffrey home to their flat, they found waiting a telegram that had arrived from America. Darnell opened it as Penny rested in the sitting room with Jeffrey in her arms, before taking him up to the nursery. "Penny, you'll like this. The telegram is addressed to you and to me. It just says, *'Hello, Sweet Prince'*. And, of course, you know who it's from . . ."

She nodded and smiled at her husband, and looked down at the little bundle in her arms. "Yes, dear. From John Barrymore."

Epilogue

Three weeks later, on Sunday, the last day of August, the Prince of Wales received John Darnell, Penny, and their new child in a ceremony at Buckingham Palace. King George V and Queen Mary were there to thank Darnell, and the King presented him with a Silver Royal Victorian Medal, proclaiming John Darnell to be a Commander in the Royal Victorian Order.

Prime Minister David Lloyd George, who took time away from his duties to attend, shook Darnell's hand and congratulated him. "Again, John, you've served England well."

The Prince of Wales drew a velvet ring box from his pocket and presented it to Penny. "This is one of my signet rings, Mrs. Darnell, one that I like and value. It's an adult size, of course, but I want you to have it for your son when he grows up. A remembrance of an occasion when his father was of service to me and your son was there—but still not quite there."

"Thank you, Your Highness. I know he'll treasure it always, and John and I will, too."

With the ceremony concluded, and led by a Palace attendant, Darnell and Penny walked down the long corridor to the front exit and left the Palace. Penny looked down at her child, then up at Darnell, and smiled. "Let's go home . . . *Commander!*"